SHOT IN THE DARK

Julie was a hell of a good looking girl, and apparently an eager one, but it's hard to make love to a woman who holds a gun to your head.

"Don't you like me at all?" she asked provocatively.

"We've just met," Shell answered.

"Can't I convince you I'm a friend? I didn't know at first, you see? I shot to warn you away. I hurt you but I didn't mean to. I still thought you were one of them, of course, but then I heard you talk to Pa. He doesn't believe you, but I do now."

"Do you?"

"Of course." She kissed each ear, her breasts swaying across his chest tantalizingly as she moved from side to side. "Don't you believe me?" she asked as a child might. She kissed his bare shoulder and her hand tightened on his thigh. He felt her throw her leg up and over his, felt the soft brush of her crotch against the muscles of his thigh as she did so.

The girl had some convincing arguments, there was no doubt about that!

SHELTER

#10
MASSACRE MOUNTAIN

BY PAUL LEDD

ZEBRA BOOKS
KENSINGTON PUBLISHING CORP.

1.

The bullet smashed into the battered body of Jeb Thornton and ripped him from the saddle. He fell, his horse going to its hind legs, whinnying in blind panic. Thornton lay unmoving, his face washed with blood, his arm broken at the elbow, his eyes open to the sun. Welton Williams was blazing away with both guns. Shelter saw him tagged, tagged again, his body jerking with the impact of each bullet. Still his guns blazed until finally a last bullet hit its mark and Williams went down, his horse trampling on him, a hoof going nearly through his rib cage.

Dinkum was frozen with panic. Blood had blinded him. His glasses lay smashed on the ground and Shelter heard himself yelling, "Run, Dink! Run for the river!"

He could hear his own voice echoing in his ears, hear the roar and thud of the guns, see the faces of those firing. The cloud of black powder smoke lay close to the earth and Shell himself fired until his gun was empty, feeling the raw, searing pain of a bullet.

Still they fired, still the guns roared and he could see he wasn't going to make it. Not this time. He bellowed a curse and sat upright in the bed. Ellie was there and she placed a cool, tender hand on his bandaged shoulder.

"Again?" she asked. "Will you dream it forever?"

He shook his head. It was dark and cool in the new house at Adobe Falls. A horse nickered far away in the paddock. Shell rose, wiping back his long dark hair. He walked to the night table and poured a drink of water which he choked down. Then he walked to the window, and drawing the curtain aside he stared out at the star rich Arizona night.

He cracked the window a bit and the cool air rushed in. Shelter stood there silently for long minutes as if he could see that last battle being reenacted out on the sleeping desert as it was reenacted, with few exceptions, nightly in his dreams.

Ellie touched him. She was naked as well and he felt her breasts against his back, felt the soft drape of her hair, the touch of her cheek against his shoulder blade.

"Come back to bed. It's over, let it be over."

He said nothing. Slowly he turned from the window, however and embraced her, pressing her softness to him. His hand slid to her smooth, taut buttocks and he held her tightly.

"It's not over, Ellie. They're not all buried."

His voice was soft but husky in the night and it was only then that Ellie knew with a certainty. Knew that Shelter Morgan would be leaving her. *They're not all buried.*

She took him by the hand and led him to the bed. Ellie lay back, her smooth flesh ivory-blue in the starlight. Her heart was pounding as he stood over her, a tall, wide-shouldered man with solemn blue eyes which swept over her body just now and smiled with delight.

She said nothing. Her hands stretched out to him, her fingers making impatient, beckoning gestures. He came to her then, the bed sagging beneath his weight, her pulse racing as he kissed her throat, her breasts.

She said nothing. There was no point in arguing with him. He was a man; he would do what he had to. She clung to him. The night grew warmer and their bodies were slick as they came together, breast and thigh, belly and cheek. Shelter's hand was on her hip, his mouth locked with hers.

She said nothing. She could not complain, scream out that she would not let him go, that he had done enough. *They're not all buried.* And so they must be buried, because while they lived they were demons clinging to his back, ugly, saber-sharp teeth tearing at him. While they lived the nightmares would continue.

And so she only clung to him in the night, her breathing increasing its cadence as he shifted, his hand resting on the damp warmth of her crotch, as she spread her thighs and he slid between them, his mouth roaming her breasts, her throat, her mouth, as she felt him enter her, felt her own muscles respond, felt the dewy welcome.

Her hands went around him, she clung to him, becoming one, feeling the strength of Shelter

Morgan, the intensity of the man, savoring his touch as he rode her through the night, as darkness drifted away, paled by the haze of the desert sunrise, as the skies colored, as her mind, her body were immersed in sensual quiet, as the terrible tension in Shelter Morgan was released at her urging. They lay together, their hearts stilling, the night becoming day, today becoming tomorrow. *Now* slowly drifting toward the past which devoured all.

Soon he would rise up, soon he would leave, but for now she held him tightly, the tears streaming down her face.

"It was that letter, wasn't it?"

"Yes." Shelter dressed slowly, and she watched him, her heart aching.

"It was from someone who knows something about . . . one of them?" Ellie sat on the edge of the bed, naked and delightful in the golden morning light. Outside they could hear Ike Byron hitching the horses to the Tanner Line stagecoach.

"Yes," Shelter answered. He shaved before the grayed mirror on Ellie Tanner's bedroom wall. Then, towelling his face, he stood silently, staring at the lean, blue-eyed face of the man in the mirror. He had picked up a scar on his face. A slanting white line which ran at an angle from the corner of his mouth to his jawline. It was something to see, to be exposed to anyone who chanced to look at Shelter Morgan. He thought briefly of the other scars, the ones no one saw.

"You are the only one who can pull this off."

The voice was that of General Custis, a tall, silver

8

haired man with green eyes and a kindly, worried smile.

"Shell?" Ellie said, but it was no good. He was back there again, back in the war.

"It's not going to be easy," Colonel Fainer said. He too smiled. "We know what we're asking."

Outside the state of Georgia lay burning. Smoke rose into the skies, shadowing all of the earth. Men lay dying under blackened trees. A soldier screamed in agony. He had no legs and no morphine to make him forget that tragedy, to numb the terrible pain, the memory of the camp surgeon—the cook with his meat saw—removing the legs while six soldiers held him down.

"Without supplies, Shell," Fainer went on, "we'll have a hundred dead of gangrene, feeling every moment of pain. We'll have a hundred more with frostbitten feet. We'll have a hundred more dead of starvation. But there is a chance. A slim, so slim chance . . . if a man could break through into Tennessee."

"That's your home, isn't it, Morgan?" Custis asked. Shelter nodded. "You're from up that way."

"Yes. From Pikeville, not a stone's throw from Chickamauga."

"And you know the lay of the land?"

"As well as any man, I suppose," Captain Shelter Morgan answered. "Is that the assignment then? Tennessee?"

"Yes." Custis placed a hand on the young captain's shoulder. "I was at Chickamauga, as you know, Morgan. We got our asses whipped. It was very bad and very sudden. We pulled out, leaving

9

much behind for the Union army. We pulled out and left, among other things—" he looked sharply at Shell, "a quarter of a milion dollars in gold, buried near Lookout Mountain."

"A quarter . . ."

"Do you know what that is, Morgan? A quarter of a million dollars worth of medical supplies, of shoes and blankets, food. What it is is the salvation of hundreds, perhaps thousands of our men who will not make it through this winter."

"We know what we're asking Shell," Colonel Fainer said. "To break through the Yankee lines, recover the gold, to return through the lines again—well, it's a task some would call impossible. But it's a job which must be attempted. And you are the man for the job."

And so he tried it. He, Jeb Thornton, Keane, Welton Williams, Dinkum. They travelled the cold high ridges at night and hid in thorny thickets in the daytime. They ate roots and berries, slept in the mud and slush, fought and silently killed Union pickets. And somehow, despite the loss of Keane who was killed by a sharpshooter, they recovered the gold, and half-starved themselves, exhausted, they returned to Georgia.

And it was there, there in that meadow surrounded by shell-blackened trees that they were met by Fainer, Custis, and eighteen other men enlisted and officers.

And it was there, when Shelter saw them in civilian clothes, their rolls on their horses, that he knew. It was only the gold that counted, only the gold.

"We've lost the war, Morgan. Any damned idiot

can see that. Now is our chance. A chance to have some sort of repayment for what we've lived through. We can go West, start again."

"And the wounded, the dying, those who are cold?" Shell asked through tight lips. There was no answer. There didn't have to be, for now he saw how it was. Let the others die, *they* were going to make a profit out of this war.

"No." Shelter shook his head. "Damn you all, no!"

And then the guns had opened up. Then the killing had begun. Then it had begun—this mad chase. Because Shelter, crawling into the brush along the river, blood leaking from his body, had sworn vengeance, sworn to find and bring to justice these criminals. Men who had killed their own kind, who ignored their own vows, who left their own men, men who looked up to them and trusted them, to die in filthy rags, to slowly starve, to sleep forever in the ice and mud of a Georgia winter.

"Shell?" Ellie was beside him again and he shook it all away.

"Was I at it again?" He held her to him briefly, kissing her soft dark hair.

"Again. You scared me last night. You were back there, I suppose. The way you thrashed around."

"Sorry. I guess I'm not much fun to sleep with," he said.

"That, I could not agree with," Ellie said with a big grin.

He had unfolded a piece of paper and now stood there staring at it as he tucked in his dark blue shirt. It was a list of names, not alphabetical, in no par-

11

ticular order. It was a list of names he had carried with him for a long while. Nearly half of them were now crossed out in red. Ellie glanced briefly at the list, saw the new red line through the name Charles Du Rose and shuddered.

"Have you ever thought," she suggested, "that forgetting about them, about what they did might be the way to shake those dreams?"

"Of course I have," Shelter answered. "But the dreams don't trouble me. They're only reminders. Reminders of the hundreds who died, reminders that I am the only one. The *only* one who can see that justice is done."

"More killing?" she asked in irritation, but he didn't bother to answer.

Ellie walked to the window, her pale blue wrapper tight around her full, competent body. She flung open the window and looked out the window, studying the old Adobe Falls Station briefly, the one which had burned and collapsed.

"Do you have to kill them?" she asked without turning around.

"We've discussed it before, Ellie," Shelter said, knowing that this was not what was bothering her. She simply didn't want him to go. "Most of them came West, changed their names and drifted into more crime. There's always been a chance for the ones I have killed. But they wanted it the way they got it."

"Doesn't it bother you?" She turned, and her eyes were bright.

"Sure." Shelter folded his paper and tucked it into the pocket of his blue shirt. He snatched his gunbelt from the back of the wooden chair and strapped it on. Ellie watched silently.

"Don't you ever . . . haven't you ever found an innocent man?"

"Once," he nodded, recalling Hugh Whistler who had been as much a fool in his own way as Shelter had been. Both had trusted Colonel Fainer.

"It's not your job!" Ellie said and Shelter turned away, seeing the sudden rush of tears. "The law . . ."

But they had been through all of that too. The law cared very little about a crime committed years ago, during the war. There was only one witness—Shelter Morgan, and the law had neither the inclination nor the motivation to spread out across the West searching for men who had scattered and assumed new identities.

"For what purpose?" one Washington bureaucrat had asked. "To bring them all back here to stand trial on a charge supported only by your accusations?"

That had dumped it squarely in Shell's lap. Find them, one by one and bring them to justice or forget it. Sleep with the hundreds of ghosts hovering over your bed, demanding revenge—if you can.

"Is that the letter?" Ellie asked, nodding at the yellow envelope on the table.

Shelter nodded. Ellie picked it up, not reading it then and there.

"Let's have breakfast," she said cheerfully. Together then they went into the kitchen where Shell stoked the iron stove. Then he sat to the table, eyes on Ellie who boiled coffee, fried ham and eggs and kept her eyes deliberately from Shell.

The coffee was good—hot and dark, and Ike Byron, the number one stage driver came in to share a cup with them.

"It'll be another half an hour, Shell," Ike said, and then he tasted boot leather—the inevitable consequence of putting your foot in your mouth. Ellie spun, nearly dropping the pan she held and her eyes were wide.

"Uh-oh," Ike muttered. "Did it again, did I?"

"It's all right, Ike," Shell said. "I guess she would have known in another minute or so."

"If you'll excuse me," Ike said, grabbing his hat. As he ducked out the door, Ellie, hands on hips, was still staring at Shell.

"Not this morning, Shell! Not now!"

"It's time, Ellie."

"But we haven't . . ." she fumbled for an excuse, anything. "The stage line isn't running to schedule yet."

"The army cleared the Apaches out, Ellie. Jeremiah Guthrie and his gang are hung or in prison. You've got four drivers and all but one of the old stations open—that's no reason."

"No," she shook her head, attempting to smile at the tall man. "But I thought . . . well, hoped that you might like to kind of stay on. We could do fine."

"I know we could," Shelter answered, and Ellie spun away, knowing that no argument would work.

She washed up and went out to stand beneath the sycamores. She was still there when the westbound for Tucson pulled out of Adobe Falls station with

14

Ike Byron working the ribbons, Shelter Morgan seated beside him, riding out of her life forever.

Ellie walked slowly back toward the house, her breathing heavy, feeling slightly hollow. Once in the house she sat to the table, and for some reason read the letter she had not looked at until now.

Shelter Morgan, Crater, Arizona.

Dear Mister Morgan,

A man named Sam Rutledge told me that you would likely be in Crater. He also told me you would be plenty interested in my problem. It involves a man you knew as James Middlesex (former major, CSA). This is a matter of life and death, and so if you can come soonest, please do so. Otherwise . . .

The rest of it was crossed out and try as she might, Ellie could not decipher it. She walked to the stove, opening it with a folded cloth. She tossed the letter in, watched it crinkle and expand as the flames devoured it. Then she watched the ashes for a minute before letting a big sigh escape.

Well, he was gone. And, Ellie had noticed that the handwriting was female. The signature was D.D. Short. But she was a female person. A female person in trouble with Shelter Morgan on the way.

"Well, D.D. Short," Ellie said to herself, "you've got quite an experience heading your way." Then Ellie smiled very slowly, very deeply. Shrugging she walked to the door, stood gazing out at the bright morning for a minute and shouted to Johnny Rojas who was filing down a horse's hoof, "The eastbound will be in soon, Johnny. Best get a team ready."

15

Johnny smiled and waved and Ellie Tanner went back into the house and began preparing the meal for the stage passengers. It was only every once in a while that she caught herself stopping, looking into the distances.

"Damn you, Shelter Morgan, I guess I'm stuck with you for a good long time." She paused and said more seriously, "Good luck to you, Mister Morgan, wherever you are going."

And good luck to anyone who stood in his way.

2.

The desert stretched out toward all horizons. Barren, brilliant, hot. The sand, like black and red glass was unbroken by vegetation. Here and there a great corrugated landform of red sandstone rose up from the sands, like the shattered remains of a beached ship. Far to the west a low line of mountains appeared as a blue, jagged line sketched against the sky. But they were so distant, so faint, as to lend the impression they were only mirage.

Shelter glanced at Ike Byron who rode slightly hunched forward, the sweat beading on his brow to be evaporated in moments by the dry blasts of desert wind.

Shelter sat back, his Winchester propped between his knees. He was not relaxed, it was no country or time tolerant of complete relaxation, but both he and Ike carried a certain confidence in them. It had been different a few months ago, with the Apache prowling and the Guthrie gang preying on the stage line.

Now it seemed that only the desert was their adversary, as it always had been, always would be. The unwary didn't last long out here.

"Where are you going from Tucson?" Ike asked above the rattle of the coach, the thudding of the horses' hooves.

"Actually I'm not going that far, Ike," Shell said. "There's a little town called Sutler's Flats just east and a little north, isn't there?"

"There is," Ike frowned, "or was last time anybody looked. Places like that—they blow away in the dry wind, the sand covers 'em up. What's there anyway?"

"I don't know," Shell shrugged. "That's where the letter came from."

"The letter?" Ike squinted at Shell. "Oh the one about . . . another one of them."

"That's right." Shell looked away across the shimmering flats. Another one of them. Major James Middlesex. Tall, taciturn, deadly. Shelter could picture him clearly in his mind despite the long intervening years. He could recall the unsmiling, long face, the blue-black hair, the dark eyes, the bloodless complexion of James Middlesex. He could recall his eye behind the sights of a death-spewing rifle as Shell's gold-bearing patrol was cut down by those greedy, self-serving men, the men who were supposed to be the leaders, the flowers of the South, knights errant for a noble cause. There was a nobler cause it seemed, gold.

"As I recall Sutler's Flats is twenty miles off the track, Shelter," Ike shouted. "I'd better swing you up that way."

"You'll get behind schedule, Ike."

18

"Hell, there wouldn't be no schedule to meet if it hadn't been for you. Ellie'd skin me if she thought I dropped you off in the middle of nowhere to try and make your way up there."

Shell smiled in appreciation. He looked around at the changing land. The shifting sun changed the shadows from moment to moment. The sands became amber and then nearly white. They passed the skulls of two oxen which still lay near the yoke. The human bones were not visible. Maybe they had made it out. Maybe.

The desert was unforgiving, and Shelter found himself longing again for the high mountains, the meadows, the green grass of Colorado where he had left so many memories.

"There's one!" Ike shouted and Shell lifted his eyes to see an Indian, mounted and motionless, far distant. The Apache, if Apache he was, sat his grulla horse atop a black basaltic outcropping, simply watching.

"That's not a man who's got his mind on warring," Shell commented and Ike agreed. Simply an Indian, watching time pass as it had too quickly for his people and their ways.

The land began to change, growing rougher and rockier then gradually rising in a series of tiers. Nopal cactus flourished here and they scattered hundreds of jack rabbits as the stage dipped down into a sandy wash and up the far side, the sun beating down on their shoulder blades.

A mile farther on, at a junction in the road where three sun-withered cottonwoods grew together, Ike swung onto the northbound trail which was overgrown with weeds, littered with rocks from the last flash flood down the shallow gorge.

They jolted over a rock and came down hard. Ike looked back at the rear right wheel and shook his head. "Thought I broke it that time. I got to remember to tell Ellie we don't want to add Sutler's Flats to the line."

They rode on through the afternoon. The sun lowered and the land was darkened by shadow, but there was no cooling. At five o'clock they rumbled into Sutler's Flats. The town seemed uninhabited at first glance. The buildings were weather-grayed, shrugging their shoulders beneath the sundown sky, watching the stage roll in with blind, glassless eyes.

"Great place to leave," Ike said as he drew his team up before a shabby building which purported to be a hotel.

"You do that then, Ike. And thanks, partner. Maybe I'll be around again one day."

"I hope so." Ike stuck out a brown, horny hand. "You ride with care now, Shell, watch the back trail."

"I will." Shell stepped down and stood, hat tipped back, looking up at Ike Byron.

"Shell?"

"Yes, Ike."

"Ellie said give you this." He tossed down a heavy leather sack, then whipped the horses mercilessly and with a loud, drawn-out "Hee-yaw!" Ike was gone, leaving only a cloud of slowly settling dust. Shelter bent down, picked up the sack and smiled.

Gold money, and she had given it to him the only way she knew he would accept it. He tucked it away, recalling her briefly, vividly. She was a hell of a gal, that Ellie Tanner. If he had any brains he would buy a horse and ride back to Adobe Falls, settle in for a summer of loving, of Ellie's good cooking, of comfort.

Shell turned, tucked the sack into his shirt and walked toward the hotel. Stepping up onto the boardwalk, wary of rot which seemed to have already gnawed at the uprights, he went on in.

It was a long wait for the room clerk who sauntered out of some musty smelling back room after Shell had been standing, propping up the ancient counter for fifteen minutes. In the meantime Shelter had signed in. He noticed that the last guest the hotel had had checked out six weeks earlier. The clerk seemed almost surprised to see a customer.

"Any chance of getting a bath with the room?" Shell asked as he scrawled his signature. The clerk looked confused. After a minute he wagged his head.

"No. There's a barber shop . . . well, he's not open after five. Tomorrow, maybe."

Shell took a rusted key from the dry hand of the clerk and walked to the corridor immediately ahead, turning right to find Number Ten.

The room was hot, airless, musty. He opened the window which overlooked a cluttered alley and sagged onto the bed for a minute. No breeze stirred outside and the room was no cooler after ten minutes than it had been.

Groaning as he rose he went to the bureau, finding the water pitcher empty. Sutler's Flats was not exactly flourishing, nor was it a place to recommend to friends. Shell rubbed his gritty eyes and pulled a fresh shirt from his bag.

Unbuttoning the old blue shirt he slipped into a fresh white cotton shirt which showed plenty of creases. Then he brushed his hair back, thought about a dry shave and decided against it, wiped his boots a little with a piece of rag and started out to find something to eat.

He didn't get far. His hand reached out, circled the brass knob of the door and found it locked. Shelter, warned by some atavistic instinct stepped to one side quickly and as he did a heavy bore rifle opened up. Three shots were fired through the door, spraying the room with flying splinter.

Shelter drew his Colt, sent four shots through the door in answer and had the satisfaction of hearing a painful groan. Backing toward the window he jammed fresh cartridges into his Colt.

The window was a bad idea. Just as he reached it a shapeless dark face appeared in the window and Shell saw the outline of a revolver by the meager light. He dove for the floor, heard the shattering roar of a .44 and he fired back.

His shots were no truer, but more effective. A bullet smashed the lower left pane of glass from the window and Shell saw a face, shards of glass imbedded in it, blood streaming down, fall back, a hand clawing at it.

He spun back toward the door as a shoulder was driven into it. The door burst open on sprung hinges and Shell fired just as a shotgun blast filled the room with jutting red flame and black smoke.

Shell felt the savage biting pain high on his shoulder, above the collarbone and he fired back.

Now they were trying the window again. He emptied his gun in that direction, hearing a shriek of pain, seeing the sash blown to jagged slivers.

He tipped over the heavy bureau and got behind it, furiously shoveling new loads into his Colt. The shotgun man had taken two steps into the room before Shell's .44 bullet tore open his chest and he died, sprawled against the floor.

Shell ducked low as guns opened up from the window. The bureau was hit again and again, but miraculously they did not hit him. Not then. His bed was shot to rags, he saw. The shotgun blast had done that. The wall behind Shell was peppered with lead.

A gunman, braver or more foolish than the rest swung a leg up over the window sill and lunged at Shell. Morgan's bullet caught him at the base of the throat and he went down in a bloody heap.

Shelter had his eyes on the window for a moment too long. From the tail of his eye he had seen movement, yet he could not identify it. Someone had entered the room from the door, however; of that he was sure. Yet in the darkness . . .

Black-powder smoke burned his nostrils, brought tears to his eyes. He blinked them away, trying to penetrate the dark confusion of his room. The bed with its white sheets he saw clearly. Was there someone behind it? He couldn't waste the ammunition to fire at it just to make sure.

He scanned the floor. Three dead, sprawled bodies. But there should not have been three!

Two. Two of them were dead men, and the third—which one was it? His head reeled with confusion. His shoulder was filled with white-hot pain. He heard another sound at the window and his eyes scuttled that way. His thumb heeled down hard on the curved hammer of his Colt, his finger twitched on the trigger. Nothing. No one.

But the bodies—something had changed, one of them had moved. But which? Shelter wiped the perspiration from his eyes, trying to order his thoughts, to recall exactly how the three bodies had lain, but he could not.

"All of them." There was only one solution, distasteful as it was. Calmly shoot each of them through the skull. It would not hurt the dead.

And then he heard a fierce cry from the window, saw a lithe, dark figure leap through, rifle firing, and Shell shot back.

And from the floor a man lunged simultaneously, steel flashing as he dove, his hand driving downward. He had a bowie and meant to use it now to destroy Shelter Morgan.

Shell slapped up reflexively with his Colt and he heard the cold clang of metal on metal. The bowie missed him completely, but his pistol was jarred from his hand.

In a cold sweat Shelter rolled away as the knife wielding man slashed back-handed at his belly, the razor sharp bowie missing by a fraction of an inch. A bullet from the window whined off the wall, narrowly missing Shelter's shoulder. He clawed frantically for his Colt and failed to find it.

The man with the knife came over the bureau and Shell kicked out with both legs, catching his assailant in the belly. The man tumbled over Shell's head and landed with a grunt.

In the faint light Shell saw the shotgun lying beneath a dead man's body and he tore it from under the man. It was empty, but as the knife hand again slashed at him, Shelter swung hard, holding the barrel of the scattergun. The stock of the weapon smashed into the hand of his attacker and he heard distinctly the sound of bone cracking.

The man howled and fell back and Shell hefted the shotgun again. This time he brought it down hard on the man's skull and he sagged to the floor.

Another one was through the window and Shell spun to face him. He swung with the shotgun, missed and saw the intense, near muzzle flash of the man's rifle. Shell felt the heat of the powder flash against his cheek and he lowered his head, diving at the man. He hit him square, his shoulder colliding with his chest and they fell together to the hard floor.

Shelter felt a fist impact with his jaw, felt the frantic writhing of the man beneath him. He swung a short, chopping right to the man's face, following with a left which only glanced off of his skull.

The other man rolled and brought a knee up hard, driving Shelter from him. Shelter stumbled over a dead body, struggled to maintain his balance and slammed into the wall. The man dove at him from out of the darkness.

He saw it then, inches from his hand. The bowie lay glittering in the feeble light and Shelter snatched it up with his left hand.

As the outlaw hit him he drove it up, feeling it go in to the haft, feeling the hot rush of blood against his fist, the death spasms of the man.

And then it was done. The room was still. When

25

Shell finally got to his feet, his chest heaving, his face trickling blood, he staggered to the lamp and lighted it.

Three men lay dead on the floor. There was a smeared trail of blood where the other had dragged himself to the window. The window itself was smashed, the frame splintered. Smoke still hung heavy in the room. The picture on the wall—an ox wagon out on the plains—was sprayed with bullets as was the wall around it. The overturned bureau was broken and perforated by buckshot. The bed had similarly been destroyed.

Shelter snatched up his Colt, his Winchester and his bag and with a cautious glance into the empty corridor, he went out of the room, his shirt in ribbons, his face bruised and bloodied.

The clerk was at the counter, his face pallid and drawn. He looked up, blinked at Shelter and asked, his voice shaking: "Something wrong, sir?"

"That room. It's a mess. I can't stay in it."

"Oh? Would you like to look at another?"

"No—you have a sheriff or town marshal?" Shelter asked.

"In Sutler's Flats! No, sir, We never have felt the need of hiring a peace officer. This is a very law-abiding community."

"Good." Shelter turned, started to go, then swung back and with all of his might back-handed the desk clerk, knocking him back into the pigeonholes behind the desk. His head jerked against the solid wood and he went out cold. Shelter picked up the register and tossed it on the unconscious clerk's lap.

Then he turned and went out into the street, easing

26

onto the shadowed boardwalk. His shoulder ached and he was wondering what they did for a sawbones around here. Recalling the barbershop, he turned that way. Likely the barber was the best they had in the way of medical help in a town this size.

He had stepped down from the boardwalk and was crossing the alley when he heard the small whisper.

"Mister Morgan!"

It was a woman and he stopped, turning that way. Still he drew his Colt. His first hour in Sutler's Flats had done nothing to make a more trusting man out of him.

She stood deep in the shadows, but even in the poor light of the alleyway Shelter could see that she was blond, young and pretty.

"Thank goodness I caught you in time." Her voice was a whisper and she gripped his sleeve. "They're after you. Somehow they found out you were coming here."

"You're D.D. Short?"

"That's right . . . why you've been in a fight!"

She looked at his bloody face, the torn white shirt, smudged with dirt, and then saw the Colt which Shelter held beside his leg. She let go of him and stepped back rapidly.

"That's right," Shelter answered. "I was in a fight. *They* found me. Now suppose we go somewhere and you tell me who they are and what you know about James Middlesex."

"I . . . of course." She swallowed so hard that Shelter could hear the gulp. "I suppose . . ."

"We'd better do it now, Miss Short," Shell said. "I don't know if they'll be wanting to try it again or

27

not, but I really don't want to hang around and find out, do you?''

"No, of course not. But, my goodness . . ." she touched her throat nervously and her eyes opened wider still. "If we . . . whatever. I don't know where . . ."

"Just out of here," Shelter said, rescuing her from her confusion. "Anywhere at all will do. I've got a buckshot pellet in my shoulder and I've got to have a look at it."

"My goodness!" she said again, now noticing the red stain on Morgan's white shirt. "Well, we should, I guess . . ."

"Now, Miss. Now, please before they catch up with me."

"I've got my buggy."

"Where?" She lifted an indicating hand and Shelter, taking her by the arm, guided her along.

The buggy, drawn by a nervous looking bay with one white stocking and his tail done up with a ribbon, stood two buildings down. Shelter helped D.D. Short up and then stepped in himself, unwinding the reins, slapping them against the haunches of the bay who moved out briskly, holding his tail high.

"He's not used to . . ." D.D. Short said, and Shelter wondered if this timid woman ever finished a sentence. "The horse, that is."

From that Shell decided that she meant the bay wasn't used to the whip, used to being hurried or used hard. He didn't bother to answer. Instead he asked where they could go.

D.D. was hesitant. She glanced at him and then quickly away, watching the sharp forms of the rising hills against the blue-black night sky. "There's my house, but of course, with you being a man . . ."

Shelter waited. She didn't finish it. Sharply he asked, "Where is your house?"

"It's across . . ." she pointed toward a grassy saddle which lay between two jagged, uptilted hills and Shelter swung the buggy that way. They rode in silence for a while.

Shelter's shoulder nagged him. He knew the wound was not serious, yet it hurt, and he was leaking blood. He was annoyed and angry. He had been attacked viciously, and it was a wonder he was not dead right now.

The bay trotted along at its own pace and the silence of the desert night enveloped them. Sutler's Flats was hidden by the hills now and there was no light but that of the stars, brilliant, cold and blue pasted against the blue-black skies.

The girl had fallen silent, maybe it was just as well. She was a shy, nervous thing apparently, upset by events, upset at the prospect of taking this man to her house. Well, maybe she had the right to be jumpy—Middlesex apparently had intruded on her life somehow, and Middlesex was a man to make anyone jumpy, if tonight's work was any indication of how the man worked.

"The left-hand fork," D.D. said quietly, "through the oaks."

Shelter swung the bay that way. They jolted down a rough, water washed road, through the ancient, black oaks and then across a small wooden bridge laid over a deep gorge. The house lay ahead of them, white against the black meadow.

It was no tiny cabin. Of two stories with a narrow

portico supported by neo-Grecian columns, the house was dark but imposing. In this part of the country it was nearly incredible to find such a house.

Everywhere was the mark of a well-run, moneyed operation. White painted paddocks and fenced pastures, a fountain, unfunctioning in the front yard, a smooth gravel driveway, a huge white silo. But there seemed to be no one around, and here and there were signs of deterioration if you looked closely enough. There was no butler to come out onto the porch and await the mistress of the house, no sign of stock in the fields, and Shelter wondered.

He guided the buggy to the front porch at D.D.'s directions, and tying the bay he followed her to the door. She fumbled with the key, looked nervously at Shelter and fumbled some more.

"Something the matter?" he asked.

"Well, it's just that . . . I was brought up in a way that . . . a man alone in the house with me, doesn't seem . . ."

"I'm harmless," Shell assured her with a sigh. "And if we don't get in sooner or later I'm afraid I'm liable to bleed to death here on your front porch."

"Oh, dear . . . of course." D.D. found the keyhole, swung the massive white door open and led the way into the interior of the great house.

The front hall was unfurnished, and it had the damp, empty smell of a room long uninhabited, long cold.

"This way." He followed her through the darkness to a second door, down another, wider corridor and into a scrubbed, white kitchen. When D.D.

had the lamp lighted, it cast smoky shadows on clean, spotless walls. The smell of cooking lingered in the air.

"I use only a small part of the house now," D.D. said, wiping back a strand of blond hair. "My bedroom upstairs and the kitchen. Everything else . . ."

By the lamplight Shell could see that she was prettier than he had expected. She had a small, nearly straight nose with flaring nostrils flanked by wide gray eyes. Her mouth was small, delicately curved. Her neck was graceful, smooth, projecting from wide, almost boyish shoulders. From there on down nothing boyish occurred.

Her breasts were full, tightly bound, her waist long and narrow. Her hips flared dramatically beneath green satin.

She caught his appraising eyes on her and she fidgeted nervously, intertwining her fingers. "I'd better boil some water, or . . . if there's any bandages . . ."

"Have you got any liquor?" Shell asked commandingly.

"I believe there's some . . . my father used to . . ."

"Get it. And bring two glasses."

"Two, but I . . . never . . ."

"You're going to start then," Shell said. He watched the girl dig in the pantry, emerge with a bottle of labeled bourbon, find two dusty glasses which she rinsed in a bucket of water and then dried. She poured Shelter three or four ounces and poured herself half that.

"A little more." Shell placed his finger on the

neck of the bottle and watched until the level of amber liquid in her glass matched his own.

He leaned back then in the straight-backed wooden chair slowly sipping the whisky, feeling the slowly spreading warmth. D.D. tasted hers hesitantly, made a wry face and then with a resigned sigh drank it down. She busied herself then starting a fire in the stove under a kettle of water.

By the time the water was boiling, D.D. had torn a clean sheet into ribbons of bandage and the whisky had settled her enough so that her sentences, if spoken in a slightly slurred drawl, at least found completion.

"Your letter said you had some sort of problem with Middlesex." Shelter winced as she pulled his shirt away from the scabbed wound. "I believe you said it was a 'matter of life and death'."

"That is exactly what it is. I'm scared, Mister Morgan. There's no law at all in this area, you know. No one to turn to."

She probed Shelter's wound and gritting his teeth he waited until she had it. The buckshot clattered out into the steel bowl she held. She clucked her tongue, cleaning the wound, examining it.

"Not so bad, I don't think," she said. A strand of yellow hair had fallen free and it brushed Shell's shoulder as she examined the wound. Her scent, faintly of violets, faintly of woman, was in his nostrils. She pulled away.

"What exactly is your problem, D.D.?" Shell wanted to know. "You think Middlesex is going to kill somebody. Who?"

"Why, me, Mister Morgan. James Middlesex is out to kill me, and there's no one to stop him. No one but you."

3.

She cleaned Shelter's shoulder with carbolic and bandaged it. She hummed softly as she worked and Shelter looked around the white and copper of the kitchen, feeling her light touch. When she was through she stood back, hands on hips and nodded with satisfaction.

"There, that should do you."

She went to clean up and Shelter watched her as she washed her hands with that strong lye soap, he watched the curve of her slender back, the set of her shoulders, the lamplight on her blond hair and wondered why anyone would want to destroy such a magnificent creature.

"I think you should tell me about it," Shelter prompted. "Exactly what is happening here? Why should Middlesex want to harm you? What is he to you, anyway?"

"James Middlesex," she said turning to face Shell, arms folded across her apron front, "was my husband—I suppose he still is legally."

"Your husband?" Shell squinted with surprise.

"Yes. He was quite charming. He dressed neatly and smelled like a gentleman. Around here that is unique enough to turn a girl's head."

"And so you married him."

"And so I did. My head was filled with stars, and I didn't believe any of the stories that drifted my way from time to time. I didn't . . . listen to my father who knew. Somehow he knew."

"Where is your father?" Shelter asked, looking around the empty room once again, listening to the silence of the old house.

"Why that's just the point, Mister Morgan." D.D. sighed heavily and waved a hand. "My father is dead—Middlesex killed him."

The girl's eyes sparkled with tears now and she wiped at her nose with the hem of her apron. Shell gave her a moment and then asked her, "Do you want to tell me about it?"

"Of course." She smiled hesitantly and then walked to the half full bottle of whisky. "I never really drink, but if you don't mind, tonight . . ."

"Sure. Hit me again too, will you?" The shoulder ached dully now and he felt a little lightheaded—he realized he hadn't eaten since breakfast. Shell accepted the glass of whisky from D.D. gratefully.

She took a drink, made a face and set the glass aside. "My father, Kenneth Short was one of the first white men in this area. There were Apaches all over the country in those days, and it wasn't the healthiest spot on earth," D.D. said. "He never meant to stay here himself. Father was passing through on his way to California. He was a shipfitter

34

and knew that men with his trade were scarce in San Francisco.

"He and an old friend, a man named Jack Shandy made camp in Cougar Pass one night. Shandy—or my father, depending on who tells it, went out looking for firewood and discovered an old dead oak which had fallen after a recent rain. My father was breaking off some small branches and the late sunlight happened to gleam on something caught in the roots of the tree.

"He took a look and found—gold clinging to the roots. High grade, jewelry grade gold. He dropped the firewood, called to Jack Shandy and they dug around the roots, finding a pocket of ore."

D.D. took another drink and then hiccupped. She blinked her eyes sleepily; the whisky was taking hold.

"They stayed on," she said. "Stayed on and started mining. It was rough at first with claim jumpers and the Indians, but gradually the town built up."

"So that's how Sutler's Flats got its start."

"No—not Sutler's Flats. That came later. The old town is up in the hills. Massacre, they named it. Massacre . . . the Apaches did come once, you see. Five Irishmen my father and Shandy had hired were killed.

"But," she paced the room now, "the mine started to pay off big and Massacre endured. My father wouldn't allow liquor or loose women in Massacre, and so Sutler's Flats was spawned. They moved in in a big way with gambling tables and bad whisky, everything they needed to separate Father's miners from their pay.

"Father built this house." She waved a hand around and sighed again, wistfully. "Eventually he pulled out of the mining operation although he still owned a half interest. There just wasn't enough ore coming out to make it worthwhile."

"How about Jack Shandy?"

"Oh, he stayed on. There were arguments—I still remember them. That little, withered, bearded dirty man standing in our front parlor telling Father that if they only poured back some of the profits into the mine it could be as rich as ever. But Father knew the mine was played out. Too often, he said, men had returned every cent they had made in hopes of finding a richer vein. He wouldn't do it and Shandy was furious. He never spoke to my father again. If they met on the streets of Sutler's Flats, they walked right past each other without speaking."

"Was your father right?" Shelter asked incisively.

The girl frowned, flapped her arms and slapped her thighs. "Not according to Shandy. He claims he's hit a new vein—fifteen years after Dad pulled out. And my Father still held fifty per cent of the claim!"

"Although Shandy had done all the work."

"Exactly. Father didn't care. He said Shandy had gone crazy years ago and anyway he wouldn't touch an ounce of the gold if there was any."

"Enter James Middlesex?" Shelter asked quietly. She turned and gave him an odd look.

"Yes." She nodded thoughtfully, finished her whisky and sagged against the table. "Enter James Middlesex. He came from nowhere, a handsome charming man, so different from the miners I'd

36

grown up around. I hated it here. Sutler's Flats is a dying town, I'm sure you noticed that," she said and Shelter nodded. "There was only the mine to give it a reason to exist, and the mine was dry—according to everyone but Jack Shandy. Massacre itself is a ghost town."

Shelter nodded his understanding. The girl had much apparently, a fine house, nice clothes, but there was nothing to do in this forsaken place, no nice young men. Middlesex must have taken her by storm.

"We were married. In the garden," she said, waving a hand toward some indefinite place behind the wall. "With flowers clinging to trellises overhead. We marched beneath them. It was a clear, beautiful day . . ." She clouded all up and had to stop.

"He changed after the wedding. He was always probing Father, asking about the mine, all the details—did he still own half of it. Father found him in his private papers once and blew his top. Middlesex just laughed. Said he was part of the family now and had a right to know about the financial situation.

"And then one day . . . Father was found near Rooster Rock. They said he must have fallen from his horse and cracked his head on a rock. But I knew. The satisfied smirk on James' face when they brought Father home told me."

After that things could only have gotten worse, Shelter guessed. Somehow Middlesex knew, or thought he knew that there was a new strike in the mine. Although Kenneth Short who should have known thought it was just the delusion of Jack Shandy—a man who had spent fifteen years and every penny he had made initially trying to prove that the mine was not played out.

Maybe Middlesex's thinking didn't go that far, however. There was a chance there was money to be made and being married cost him nothing—the girl could always be dumped later—and so he took the chance. At the least he would end up with this house and all the land Kenneth Short owned.

Or would he? Shelter asked D.D. about it. She was extremely weary now. The alcohol had numbed her, made her eyelids heavy.

"He didn't come in for any of it," she replied in answer to his questions. "Father's will was quite specific. The interest in Shandy's mine, the house, all came to me, of course, but Middlesex was barred from owning any of it, from attempting to sell anything . . . unless, of course . . ."

Unless of course D.D. was also to die unexpectedly, quite accidentally. Shelter nodded. D.D. seemed unable to go on with her story. Weariness apart, she had stirred up too many old demons and she was frightened, truly and deeply frightened.

"You need some rest, D.D. There's no chance of Middlesex coming here tonight?" He asked almost hopefully. That would bring it all to a swift, violent conclusion.

"No," she shook her head. "Or at least I don't think so. I've heard he was in Tucson, trying to break the will, I think. Who knows with James," she shrugged, "but I don't think he'll be back tonight."

"I'll lock the doors and sit up," Shelter offered.

She smiled gratefully and told Shelter goodnight.

He watched her go off up the corridor, the lantern casting a changing globe of light around her, making her appear somehow smaller, more frail.

There was much he still wanted to know, but tomorrow would do. His main concern now was where Middlesex was. If he had gone to Tucson to try to break the will, he had probably failed. It seemed unlikely any judge, no matter how shady would take it upon himself to set aside the terms of Short's will. If that was so, then that left Middlesex with only one alternative, and D.D. knew it. She would have to be done away with.

Knowing Middlesex he would have no qualms about it either.

Shelter's eyes had adjusted to the dim light of the empty house now and he walked through the hallways, crossing the imposing reception room, to the front door.

He peered out and stepped onto the porch, listening to the night sounds, watching the starlit skies for a long while. He could see no lights from Sutler's Flats, no light anywhere across the broad land. The desert flats far beyond the broken hills showed as a deep blue glassy lake. A coyote howled dolorously somewhere and was answered. A faint breeze stirred the old oaks across the yard. Otherwise it was still, dry and cool.

Shelter went back in, slipped the bolt and took up a seat in the parlor. He sank into the plush red chair, feeling the stiffness in him now. The fight had taken a toll.

He sat with his rifle across his thighs, and he wondered. Wondered how Middlesex had known he was coming, wondered how—if James Middlesex was in Tucson, he could have arranged the hotel attack.

He sat there, fighting off the whisky and the weariness, trying to stay awake in the stillness of the empty house.

It was sometime after midnight when he came suddenly alert. He had heard something—or imagined he had. Some small sound which did not belong in the night. Frowning he rose stiffly from the chair and crept to the curtained window.

He looked out at the yard which was now glassy with dew. Nothing. He turned away from the window, and deciding abruptly, crossed the room and went toward the kitchen. He passed on through the still warm room and found the back door locked.

Opening it a hair he looked out and then went through, drawing the door shut behind him silently. Nothing. Probably imagination working overtime, he decided, but it nagged him.

He stepped off the back porch, a plank creaking underfoot, and into the darkness of the yard. He walked to the corner of the house, his rifle cool in his hand. He eased around the corner. Nothing. No one.

He was beginning to feel a fool, but he had learned long ago that in battle it was best to take nothing for granted. Too many sentries had ignored the bird whose song wasn't quite right, been reluctant to leave the fire to investigate a shadow where no shadow had been.

The night was cool. Shell began to shiver as he moved at a half crouch toward the front of the house. He stopped abruptly.

That time it was definite—a sound where none should have been. He crouched lower, hugging the shadowed side of the house, trying to identify the sound; and then he had it—the creaking complaint of rusted hinges.

He could see the dim outlines of an outbuilding standing in the shadows of the trees, and as he looked he could see that the door stood slightly ajar.

Slowly he drew back the hammer of his Winchester and taking a deep breath he dashed soundlessly across the space between the two buildings and pressed himself up against the wall of the shed, his heart pounding.

He stood there for long minutes, but there was no other sound. There didn't need to be—Shelter knew there was something living inside the outbuilding. He could almost feel the presence. And he had the idea that whoever, whatever it was knew he was there as well.

He crept to the door, using the muzzle of the rifle to swing it open a few more inches and then a few more. He smothered a curse as the hinges squealed again.

He waited, counting to ten, and then slipped through the door, moving quickly to one side, going to his knee as he waited, expecting the sudden explosion of gunfire.

Nothing. The shed was silent, smelling of old leather and oil, of sawdust and of rotted straw. Shelter slid along the wall, his eyes combing the darkness.

It was very dark in the shed but now Shelter could make out the general shape of things. There was a

41

workbench along the wall to his left, a few bulky undefinable objects on it. To his right was a sort of loft and before him what was probably a plow left in the center of the packed earth floor. Above and opposite his position was a narrow window, darkened with grime, and it was through there the only illumination fell. Dim starlight which shadowed all objects with imagined menace.

Suddenly imagination took life and form and as Shelter wheeled a man hurled himself out of the darkness. Shell spun that way, felt the impact of a body against his, felt his rifle slapped aside and a warm, vise-like hand against his throat.

Shelter let himself go back, falling with the impetus of his attacker. He slammed back against the floor of the shed, knocking the wind from his lungs with a rush. Yet he did not pause. Instead he kicked up and rolled, throwing his opponent over his head. Shelter heard the grunt of surprise and pain as the man landed hard on the back of his head.

Shelter spun and tried to come to his feet, but the man was a big cat. Wild, strong, sure. He took Shelter by the right wrist and the throat, his knee coming up hard and fast.

Shelter caught the knee on the inside of his thigh and fought back. The clawing hand had a hold on his windpipe and already the room was beginning to spin. Shell brought his left hand up and hammered down on the arm of his attacker.

The hand fell away and Shelter kicked out blindly, feeling with satisfaction, his bootheel land solidly on the other man's shinbone.

It didn't even slow him down. He was a hard, lean

man and he was quick. Too quick. He shrugged off the jolting kick and leaped at Shell again, mauling him like a cougar.

Shell fought back viciously, but the man was agile and powerful. He brought a right hand up hard into Shell's ribs. A stunning blow which stopped Morgan in his tracks. Then, with the precision of a skilled wrestler he moved in. Two hands shot out, gripped Shelter's shirt and although Morgan could see it coming, he could do nothing to prevent himself from being yanked off-balance. He felt a solid hip impact with his thigh and he tumbled through the air, thrown perfectly with a hip roll.

Shell hit the ground and kept rolling. He came to his feet in time to parry a slashing right hand, but then he was suddenly backheeled. He felt his boot go out from under him and he grasped at the man before him. He caught something around his attacker's neck, felt it tear free in his hand and then he thudded to the earth, cracking his head against the wall of the shed.

His brain went hot and then cold. Blue and gold pinwheels spun briefly behind his eyes. The man hovered over him and Shelter thought briefly that he had bought it.

But abruptly the man turned and on cat feet, scuttled to the door and was gone. Shelter heard the squeak of the door, saw the dark shadow move out into the yard, but he was helpless to pursue the man.

He tried to rise, nearly blacked out and had to sag back against the wall, his head reeling, his stomach turning over once.

Minutes passed and he sat there, hearing the far

distant sound of a horse running. He started to rise finally, and he felt something in his hand. He couldn't make it out in the darkness, but it was a necklace of some sort from around the throat of his attacker.

Getting to hands and knees Shelter finally rose, using the wall to support his weight until the dizziness subsided. He staggered to where his rifle lay, picked it up and went out into the cold, empty yard. The scent of dust lingered there.

He returned to the house, feeling subdued. Whoever that man was, he was damned good. In fact, Shelter considered, he was probably good enough to have killed him. But he did not, did not apparently want to.

One thing was certain then—it was not James Middlesex, had it been Shelter would still be lying in that shed in a dark pool of his own blood.

Shell went into the house, locking the door again. Stumbling to the kitchen he took a rag, dipped it in water and sat in a chair, holding the cloth to his face which was rubbed raw along one cheekbone.

Through a fog he realized that he still held the object torn from the man's throat in his hand and now he lay it on the table. It was a necklace, and quite obviously it was an Indian-made article.

Thinking back, remembering the way his assailant had fought—the hiproll, the back heeling—he had the strong suspicion that the man was an Indian. But what Indian. Why? He would ask D.D. in the morning, maybe she could shed some light on this.

Meanwhile Shelter rose and dug around in the pantry aided by a candle he had found and lighted,

44

until he found a sack full of coffee beans. He located the grinder on a counter and started the water boiling. It was going to be a long watch, he might as well make the most of it.

Propped up by the coffee he stayed awake the night long, making a circuit of the house and yard from time to time, but there were no more incidents.

When dawn broke with a silent, brief explosion of color against the eastern horizon, he heard D.D.'s footsteps on the stairs, and a minute later she appeared, her face slightly puffed with sleep, her mouth gaping in a tremendous, unladylike yawn which she tried futilely to hide behind her fist.

"Sorry," she apologized, barely suppressing another yawn. "Do I smell coffee?"

"Yes, you do," Shell said with a smile. "I'll get you some. Plant yourself."

She did so, sagging into a chair across the table from Shelter Morgan. He placed a steaming cup of coffee before her and she glanced up with a smile of gratitude. "I'm sorry," she apologized again, "but I was—am—so tired. I don't think I've slept for a week, never knowing when he would come back. Between that and the whisky . . ."

"Drink your coffee," Shell urged. Her eyes were now on the Indian necklace which lay on the table. It was made of alternating turquoise beads and beads of onyx, spaced with cylinders of silver.

"Where did that come from?" she asked.

"Have you ever seen it before?"

"No." She turned it in her fingers and shrugged, her eyes meeting those of Morgan. "Where did it come from?"

"Just something I found," he said. No need telling her she had had a prowler. Shelter was watching her fingers as they touched the beads. His eyes traveled up from her hand to her slender arm, followed the arm to her shoulders which were concealed poorly beneath a flimsy pink wrapper. Then he studied her throat, the gentle upthrust of her cleavage. When he reached her face those gray eyes were staring at him with something approaching fear and Shell let his gaze slide away. This was no time, no woman to be thinking thoughts about. She was scared, wary of men, alone and vulnerable.

Still, a man couldn't help admiring the terrain. He stood. "More coffee?"

She shook her head and got to her feet, holding her wrapper together at the throat. "I'd better get dressed," she said.

"Do that. Then, D.D., we've got some more talking to do," Morgan said.

He stood as well. She looked up at him, her golden hair, the color of sunlight, streaming across her shoulders. She smiled, and then the smile fell into a hesitant, wavering line and she took two quick steps and was against him, her breasts heaving, her face buried against his chest.

"Oh, Shelter, Shelter . . . what am I going to do? What? He'll come back, he'll kill me, I know it."

"He won't hurt you," Shelter said softly. His hand was at her waist, feeling the flex of her back muscles through the silky fabric of her nightdress. "I promise you he will not hurt you, D.D."

She stepped back, snuffling and wiping her eyes. "I guess that was overdue," she said. "There's been

46

no one to talk to. It's been terrible, never knowing . . ." she paused and Shelter thought she was going to start crying again.

"Get dressed," he said a little roughly. "Have you got any laying hens?"

"Out back. There's a chicken coop."

"Good. You get dressed. I'm going to find as many eggs as possible and whip them into something resembling breakfast."

"I couldn't eat."

"You've got to, lady," Shell said with a faint smile. "Don't let the bastard starve you on top of everything else. Dress and we'll talk. We've a whole lot of talking still to do."

"Yes," she said, "all right." She turned then to go, but just for a moment her eyes lingered on the string of Indian beads which lay still on the table. Her eyes lingered, flickered with some intelligence and then went dull again, and he was sure, sure that she knew something about them, something she was not willing to tell.

"That is going to make it real hard, lady," Shelter said to himself as she left the room. "If you start holding out on me."

He had to know it all, know what he was up against here, and if D.D. was going to try to hide something, to color the facts it might lead to both of them being found dead somewhere, accidentally killed.

There was something wrong here, something Shell could not put his finger on, but he meant to get it straight. He had a feeling that if he didn't he might as well put a gun to his own head and pull the trigger. If James Middlesex ever got hold of him, that might seem a pleasant alternative.

"Don't lie to me, Lady D.D.," he said under his breath. "If you do, woman, I'm afraid we've both bought it."

4.

When Miss D.D. Short reappeared an hour later she was wearing a white cotton blouse and a divided buckskin riding skirt.

"Good," Shelter remarked, looking up from what was his fourth cup of coffee in as many hours, "you're all ready."

"Ready?" Her eyes reflected puzzlement. "What do you mean? Ready for what?"

"Ready to leave. We can't stay here. I don't think that's wise at all. Middlesex is bound to find out where I am. He already knows where you are. If he finds us here, well, I don't think there will be much of a chance for us."

"But this is my home!" D.D. protested. She looked around her kitchen, defeat in those gray eyes.

"It was your home," Shelter said. He sat opposite her, taking her hand in his two. "Now it is a prison, a trap. You can't stay here. You'd be better off going East, out of the country if you have people there."

"No," she said, her voice shaky, "there's no one." Her hand gripped his tightly. "I never thought of leaving. It seems a terrible thing to do."

"It might mean survival."

"Yes, I can see that now." She shrugged, a tiny, helpless shrug. "I'll get a few things packed."

D.D. stood and Shell slowly released her hand. She set her shoulders, smiled and then turned away, walking from the room. Shelter watched her go, wondering what he was getting her into. Where would they go? Although it was true that Middlesex and his gang could easily destroy them if they stayed in this house, it would be equally hard to survive out there . . . he looked to the window.

It was a hard, gaunt land which shimmered in the morning sunlight beyond the window of the kitchen. Broken, rocky hills, grassless and treeless. A land of deep ravines, dry arroyos, blazing hot in the daylight hours, freezing at night. And still the Apache prowled the land in this corner of Arizona.

But Shelter had never liked being cornered and that was the situation at present. They were trapped in this house. Shell wanted to be able to move around, to pick his own field of battle.

She returned in minutes with a hastily packed cotton bag in her hands, a brave set to her shoulders, a determined smile on her lips.

"Ready?" she asked and Shelter nodded. He had already ransacked the cupboards of the house, taking what food he could use. He had only to snatch up his rifle and hat and then they were ready.

Besides the bay which was used for the buggy, there was only one other horse on the place.

"It was my father's horse," D.D. said.

It must have been Kenneth Short's horse for a good many years. The animal stood watching them warily from the paddock. An off-white gelding, perhaps ten or twelve years old, he had gone to fat. His coat was hairless in some spots and looking more closely Shelter discovered ring hoof on the right front leg.

"Poor old bastard," Shelter said. He patted the animal's neck and threw a saddle over its back. The horse rolled its eyes as if enduring a great indignity.

"His name's Cornelius," D.D. said. She watched as Shelter led the old white horse around the enclosure, watching its gait. "I'm afraid he's getting on in years."

"Well, none of us is as young as he used to be," Shelter said. He swung aboard, feeling the horse shudder beneath him. He smiled for D.D., but Shelter liked none of this. He could imagine trying to outrun pursuit on this old bag of bones.

The bay was even more of a problem. A pampered pet, used to the buggy it pulled to Sutler's Flats once a week or so, the horse wanted no part of a saddle.

Shelter mounted the bay, felt the animal go rigid and then suddenly, coiling its muscles, break into a crowhop. The bay spun and bit at his leg, kicking up dust across the corral. D.D. looked on with sympathetic eyes as Shelter broke the bay to the saddle.

Finally they were ready, ill-mounted, but mounted as well as possible under the circumstances. D.D. took the bay which responded to her touch better than it had to Shell's. It still wore a pink ribbon in its tail as they rode from the Short ranch, and from time to time the bay tried to get near enough to Morgan to nip his leg.

D.D. knew the country well apparently. She had described a small teacup valley where there was grass for the horses, an overview of the land and a gurgling spring with sweet water. There, with any luck, Shelter hoped to be able to safely conceal D.D. and come up with a reasonable method of attacking this problem.

He let D.D. lead the way. The bay stepped nimbly up a rock strewn path toward the blank faced chocolate hills above the Short Ranch. Now and then they glimpsed Sutler's Flats, far below them, tiny as a matchbox town.

When they left the Short Ranch it had been warm, ninety degrees plus and still. Now as they rode higher the temperature had dropped considerably, and Shelter knew they were in for some cold nights.

The wind picked up. It whistled up the long canyons, a dry, forceful animal, plucking at their clothing, throwing dust into their eyes.

D.D. rode on silently and Shelter followed her, trusting to her knowledge of these hills. The old white horse labored beneath him and Shelter wondered anew what would happen if he had to depend on the horse to run him out of trouble.

The hills sharpened and thrust higher against the clear pale blue sky. Now they encountered scraggly, wind-flagged cedar among the nopal and manzanita which clotted the hillsides. Higher up still Shelter could see scattered spruce, blue against the rust red earth of the higher peaks.

Those were true mountains. Shelter had met

people who thought of all of Arizona as being flat and sandy. It took some time to explain to them that there were a dozen great ranges traversing the territory. Webb Peak, visible across the distant flats rose to ten thousand feet and Mount Lemmon which stood directly ahead of them, like a shadowed bulwark, rose to nine thousand.

Gradually the trail they rode flattened and widened and Shelter let Cornelius drift up beside the bay which had settled some, the long climb putting out some of its fire.

"You never did tell me how you happened to write to me, D.D.," he said.

"Well, it was because of Sam Rutledge, of course," she explained. The wind twisted her golden hair, fanning it across her face. "He was a friend of yours, wasn't he?"

"Yes. Sam is a good man." Shell had to smile. Rutledge was a friend. He was also one of the biggest rascals West of the Mississippi. A card sharp, a patent medicine salesman, a land promoter, he was a wide eyed innocent to the uninitiated, a devil incarnate to those who had dealt with him.

But there was nothing malicious about Sam. He simply believed in making money, and doing whatever it took to do so. He and Shelter had met in a rigged poker game when Shelter had been passing through El Paso. Rutledge was the one who had been doing the rigging.

Shelter had told him the facts of life and Rutledge had returned the money to his marks, making pained faces the whole time. Part of that was due to the fact that Shelter Morgan was standing behind him, jab-

53

bing him with a persuading Colt. Shell always thought that the idea of actually handing back money was by far more painful to Sam Rutledge.

The men, as unalike as any two men, had grown to be friends. Sam was completely trustworthy as long as money wasn't involved. One night Morgan had told the gambler his story and Rutledge, deeply impressed, had asked for a duplicate list of names. Sam had promised to let Shell know if he ever ran across any of them on his wanderings, and he had on two previous occasions.

This time he had run into James Middlesex.

"What happened to Sam?" Shelter wanted to know.

"Happened to him?" D.D. repeated. "Nothing as far as I know. He worked his game in Sutler's Flats until he had run out of customers—he had some hair restorer he was peddling and there were only so many bald men. Then, I guess, he took the road west. He talked about Tucson."

"How did you happen to meet him?"

They had reached a fork in the road and D.D. indicated the proper trail with a nod of her head. Shell noted with satisfaction that there were no signs of recent usage on this trail which wound up through a small stand of pines perched on a rocky outcropping before dipping down into a canyon where a threadlike stream trickled past, then climbing again toward the high mountains where timber, blue-gray in this light colored the craggy slopes.

"I had no idea who he was," D.D. said. They rode in the shade of the pines now. A jay hopped from branch to branch, following them at a distance.

"But I heard a man asking about James Middlesex in the emporium in Sutler's Flats. Needless to say, I was interested. I managed to ask him why he wanted to know and he smiled and said he and Middlesex had a mutual friend.

"Somehow, I don't quite recall agreeing to it, we decided to have supper together at the hotel and I started talking. Lord, did I talk—it had been quite a while since I'd been able to talk to someone. Mister Rutledge listened quietly until I was through, then he said I should write to you. He said he wasn't quite sure where you were, but he imagined you were in Crater if you were still alive.

"I asked him what he meant by that but he only laughed. He said you had ridden with luck so long that you probably were invincible. Anyway, he said, it wouldn't hurt to write to you, and so I did. Rutledge drifted on, I suppose. Probably still selling that hair restorer."

"Or ice to Eskimos," Shell said with a smile.

"That too," D.D. laughed. "The man has a silver tongue."

"Yes he does," Shelter replied, but his mind was not on his reply. He had seen a glint of light on some reflective surface a mile or so back and now he had caught a clearer look. Without seeming to his eyes had searched the mountain slopes opposite them and now he was sure. They were being followed.

And unless he was very much mistaken it was an Indian.

From time to time he glanced that way, but he saw him no more. At noon he and D.D. found the camp she was looking for. Sunlight streamed through the pines, warming the long grass which grew in a park surrounded by a horseshoe of trees. Blue and yellow flowers dotted the long grass. Mountain lupine and yarrow which lined the path of the silver, twisting rill which meandered across the small meadow.

"Its source is over there," D.D. said, and they rode that way, finding a bubbling, icy spring which gurgled up from the heart of the mountain. They let the horses drink from this artesian flow and then picketed them in the long grass.

D.D. wanted to bathe and so Shell left her at the spring. He himself took a long slow circuit of the hilltop, watching the peaks opposite them, studying the backtrail. He saw no one, no flash of color, no rising dust, but only deep, beautiful valleys surrounded by majestic mountains, and far in the distance the white expanse of the wide desert.

They prepared a lunch of ham, panbread and coffee while low, ragged clouds scudded toward them from off the northwest. They sat close together, eating in silence, watching the wind play in the long grass and set the pines to rhythmic swaying.

An eagle floated high in a lonesome sky and they followed it with their eyes, envying it its effortless freedom.

After eating D.D. washed the dishes and Shelter, expecting a cool night, got to work building a lean-to out of pine boughs. There was a definite, cold edge to the wind now and D.D., finished with her cleanup, helped Shelter at his work, shivering as she did so.

They hardly spoke that afternoon. Each was busy with his own thoughts. What D.D.'s were Shelter could not have said, for himself he was planning, planning the destruction of a killer.

He took another tour of the mountain top before turning in, but he saw nothing, no movement or shape which did not belong to the wilderness.

It was already dusk, the high clouds were crimson, edged with gold. The shadows had crept out of their night hiding places and inched down the long valleys. The distant desert still gleamed with shimmering white light.

D.D. was waiting for him as he approached through the falling darkness. Her blond hair was down around her shoulders. She wore a blanket against the chill of evening. The fire was burning low and would soon be out—Shelter didn't want to risk a fire at night.

"Well?" she asked.

Shelter shook his head, pouring himself the last cup of tepid coffee. "Nothing," he replied, sitting beside her in the lean-to. "If they're out there they're quiet as cats."

"But—you saw something, didn't you? Earlier."

"Thought I did," he shrugged, "but you know how that is when you're a little jittery."

She nodded, half convinced. The pale glow was gradually fading from the sky and as they watched a single star blinked on. The wind ruffled the ranks of pines surrounding their lonely camp. Shelter finished the coffee and made to rise.

"Where are you going?" she asked. Her hand fell on his shoulder. Looking down he saw wide, nearly bewildered eyes and he wondered if he had made a mistake bringing such a creature into the wilderness.

She was wholly unsuited for such adventures.

"I thought I'd better keep watch, D.D."

"But you didn't sleep last night," she objected.

"No, but I'd feel better keeping watch. I'd rather go sleepy than have them find me in my bed."

"For just a little while then," she said in a soft, misty voice. "Stay with me for just a minute. It's cold out here . . . so cold."

She suddenly threw her arms around him. It was a child's embrace, frightened, lonely. She clung to him for long minutes as Shell watched the fire burn out, watched the stars clot the empty sky.

He could feel her breast rising and falling as her breath came spasmodically. He felt the soft brush of her fine hair against his cheek, the kneading of her fingers against his shoulders. It was a long while before he said, "I'd better get out there now."

"All right." She sat up, seemingly more in control now. "I'll sleep for a while. Then wake me up and I'll stand watch."

"You can't."

"I can shoot."

"There's more to it."

"All right," she said, her lower lip thrust slightly forward in a determined pout, "you tell me what to do then, where to stand watch. You can't go another entire night without sleeping. It's foolish, Shelter Morgan, and you know it is."

He turned it over in his mind. He did know it was foolish. Tomorrow he would be riding blind-eyed with exhaustion. It wasn't smart to take the edge off that way; it would only leave him in bad shape when he did run into James Middlesex and needed to be alert. Still . . . there was something so helpless about the woman.

"All right," he agreed just to end the discussion. He figured he would have time to think it out as he stood watch, and if he thought he could handle it he would just let her sleep.

She was satisfed with his reply and D.D. lay back and curled up. Shelter covered her with his own blanket and she smiled gratefully.

Then, picking up his rifle he moved out into the darkness. The wind was washing over the mountain in cold waves. The grass, dark in the night, shivered and was flattened by its force.

Shelter moved to the horses, yanked their picket pins and moved them uphill, closer to the camp, onto new grass.

Then, filtering through the trees where it was warmer and he was less visible, he made a circuit, pausing from time to time to listen to the wind sounds, to study the deep, cold shadows which pooled under the pines.

Nothing at all. He yawned and moved on, his eyes gritty, his body feeling slightly leaden. D.D. was right—he couldn't take another day of this. But then he knew something she didn't. There was someone following, and it was not imagination as he had pretended.

Someone. An Indian he thought. The same Indian he had grappled with in the shed? Or another. Someone tracking them for Middlesex? That made a lot of sense in a way. If Middlesex had in fact gone to Tucson, wouldn't he have left someone to keep an eye on his lovely wife?

Shelter stopped at the fountain head and drank from the icy spring, washing his face with the water which tingled on his skin and brought him momentary, spurious alertness.

He withdrew to a stack of rounded boulders higher up the slope, in the shadows of the pines and he squatted on his heels, watching the silent, dark valley. He nearly toppled over from sleepiness and angrily he got to his feet. He had to stay on the move to stay awake.

He circled back toward the trail's end, watching the sky slowly darken to the north. The clouds which had been sheer, ragged, now bunched together, towering into the skies to blot out the stars with their bulk.

It would rain, damnit. He was beginning to wonder if all of this wasn't foolish. But what else was there to do? He couldn't leave D.D. alone, he couldn't expect to hold off Middlesex in her house or in Sutler's Flats which had proven itself to be a very unhealthy spot.

He was at the head of the trail and he looked down the zig-zag shape of it as it looped and dropped into the lower valley, seeing nothing. He could detect no scent of dust on the air, could see no glow of fire. There was only the still night, the ranks of pines huddled together against the cold, the wind and the high promise of a bright star.

Shelter was staggering as he worked his way back over the broken ground to camp and he knew that reluctant as he was to do so, he would have to wake D.D. and let her sit watch.

She still slept deeply when he returned and he placed a hand softly on her shoulder.

She spun instantly, her eyes wide. Then, half-sitting she stopped, blinked her eyes fully open and smiled.

"It's you," she said and he nodded. Her hair had spun itself into a tangled golden web. An errant beam of starlight danced in her eyes.

"I'm going to have to take you up on your offer."

"All right." She threw her blankets aside and started pulling on her boots.

"There's a place near the spring where you can see most of the valley, enough to know if anyone's making a try for the horses."

"Or you?"

Shelter nodded. "Or me. Take my rifle and . . . you did say you can shoot?" he asked.

"I can shoot, and if anyone tries for you, they'll be sorry," she said with determination. Shelter smiled and went on, explaining where the boulders were, how she might best stay alert, shift position from time to time. She took it all in, nodding gravely like a child given a small task.

Shell was still uncertain. D.D. was a frontier woman, but she had been raised in town, having things done for her. Still, it would only be for four hours and Shelter himself believed the area was clear.

He watched her go, carrying his Winchester. When he could see her no more he lay back and with utter weariness drew the blankets up over his shoulders, rolled onto his side and slept.

Even as he slept he thought of D.D., however. He had ceased to worry about her, knowing that it could do no good anyway now that the decision had been made. But there was a warmth to the blankets left by her body, a faint lingering scent which worked its way into his dreams and brought them vividly to life.

It was the warmth which awakened him. It was so warm that he tossed a blanket aside drowsily. And then Shelter was aware of water dripping onto his hand. He pried an eye open and lay watching the silver beads of water drip from the slanted roof of the lean-to to splatter against the earth near his hand.

He sat bolt upright, suddenly alert, his heart hammering.

It was full day outside and it was raining. A wall of gray clouds hung across the valley, webbed between the mountain peaks and a slow steady rain was falling.

He grabbed his hat and snatched up his gunbelt. He had slept, had to have slept eight hours at least. Then where was D.D.!

He stepped out into the rain and walked swiftly across the meadow toward the springs. Probably she was only trying to be considerate and let him sleep. Probably—but Morgan was worried. Damn the girl!

The trees appeared suddenly from out of the clouds, tall, silent, glistening with rain. He scrambled up the slope and found the spring and the jumble of boulders.

She was gone.

Frantically Shelter cast about, not daring to call out, failing to make sense out of her tracks in the damp pine needles.

Likely she had gotten tired of sitting there and had decided to make a circuit, knowing that Shelter had done the same.

Grinding his teeth he left the timber and walked

back hurriedly to the camp. Better to be mounted if he was going to have to search for her. He walked through the screen of clouds, his shirt plastered to his back by the rain which now fell harder, obscuring vision.

The horses were gone. Gone! Maybe she had moved them—his saddle was still where he had placed it, across a dry log, in the shelter of the trees, but hers was gone.

Worse and worse. Why had she taken the horses? Why take both of them?

He stood there simmering for a time, looking upslope and down, and then he saw something which chilled his blood. He took a step nearer and then hunkered down.

A bootprint, neither his nor D.D.'s. It was much too large for hers. Someone then had taken the horses, someone then . . . had D.D.

He returned to the lean-to, hastily packed a small sack of essentials and rigged a rope which he used to sling it over his shoulder.

Then slowly, in the driving downpour, he set out to make a circuit of the hills. There was always a chance that she had hidden out, that they had not found her. But it was a small chance and as the hours bled by, as the rain swept down the chance grew infinitesimal.

He stood there on the rain washed mountain peak knowing that Middlesex had his wife, knowing what he would do to her if it became necessary. Knowing that it was all his own careless fault.

5.

The rain drove down all day. By mid-afternoon it was a lightning-filled, thunder-laden sky. The wind shivered the trees, and Shelter plodded on.

He had searched the timber minutely, turning up nothing. He had then returned to where the horses had been picketed and tried to pick up their trail. He managed to make half a mile over the next hour, but already he knew it was hopeless. The rain was erasing the tracks, covering all sign of passage and they were much too far ahead of him anyway.

What now? He stood in the shelter of the pines, shivering with the cold and damp, watching lightning arc between two craggy peaks as a tremendous rumble of thunder rolled down the mountain slope.

The answer, painful as it was, seemed to be to return to Sutler's Flats and the Short Ranch, although he would be lucky to make it in a week if this kept up.

He thought suddenly of Massacre. The ghost town was much closer than Sutler's Flats. Less than a day's walk by D.D.'s description. There was a chance he could get a horse there. Ghost town it might be, but Shandy was operating up there, and he must have mules at least.

The rain rolling down out of the skies now in heavy waves decided Shelter. By the time he could walk to Sutler's Flats—assuming he could make it at all in this weather—too much time would have passed. Too much for D.D.

It might already be too late for the girl, but Shelter didn't allow himself to dwell on that. Instead he turned westward, toward the high mountains, toward Massacre.

He walked on through the day, pausing at mid-afternoon for cold biscuits and boiled coffee. The rain had settled in real well, and the gorges now were alive with brawling white-water rapids.

An hour before dusk it was dark as a coal mine at midnight and Shelter was anticipating unhappily a night out in this rain. He had some luck—quite accidentally he stumbled across an old rutted road overgrown with weeds and he reasoned that it could only lead to one place in this country, to Massacre.

He turned onto the road and marched steadily upward through the whine of the storm until it became too dark to risk going any farther. Then he made camp, a miserable cold camp back under the trees, the mocking wind prodding him awake the night long.

He awoke with a start sometime after midnight. It was still raining but through a gap in the clouds a lone star shone coldly from out of a black, miniature sky.

What had awakened him. . . ? He heard the snuffling guttural sound again and by the faint light saw the rolling shoulders, the tremendous haunches of a black bear nudging his pack with its slavering muzzle.

He didn't want to shoot for two reasons. One, even above the sounds of the storm it was possible someone would hear the shot and locate him. Two—it would have to be a dead shot. There is nothing on earth more dangerous than a wounded bear.

Still Shelter drew his Colt and cocked it, and at the sound the bear's head swivelled toward Shell. There was a tense moment while the bear's slow mind untangled things and then, perhaps catching Shell's scent and not liking it, it turned bawling away from the pack and ambled off into the dark forest.

With the dull gray light which passed for dawning, Shelter was off and walking again. The trail wound higher into the mountains. On the peak opposite, visible through the parting gossamer veil of clouds, Shell could see where the timber had been cleared. Yanked free, cut hastily so that the stumps were five feet high. Timber for the mines, for the sluice boxes, the saloons of a gold town, cut in the raging ambition of gold fever.

It was an ugly sight, but one which nature, given time would smother with her cunning rebirth. Shelter stopped cold, his thoughts broken off.

He darted into the timber, holding his Colt beside his ear. Something . . . he had seen a bit of color which did not belong, a shadow suggesting a man.

Nothing moved but the trees in the wind. Cold

rain dropped off the trees and skittered down Shell's neck. He crept toward the color—a few square inches of crimson belonging to nothing of nature.

Peering through the rain he saw it again and now he slowly lowered his gun. It hung in the branches of a tree, perhaps drawn there by a mountain lion. It was a body, the body of a man.

He holstered his Colt and went nearer, his boots soundless across the bed of damp pine needles. The head, decomposed, the hide torn away in chunks, rested on the ground ten feet from the tree and downslope.

The body of the man dangled upside down from a tangle of boughs. The flash of red had been a silk cravat which was pinned to a faded, decomposed shirt with a horseshoe stickpin.

Shelter went nearer, turning the skull over with his foot, already knowing, knowing the man from the stickpin and the tie. It was Sam Rutledge.

"Old Sam," Shelter said with an empty smile. He saw something green in the needles and he uncovered it. A small square bottle of hair restorer, its label peeled by time and dampness.

"You didn't fill this straight, did you Sam?" He stood, staring down with affection and disgust at the remains of what had been a good man.

Sam was a clown, a huckster, a devil-may-care, lady-hunting, dapper little man with a streak of the larcenous and a fast shuffle. Yet he had been a friend, a good friend to Morgan.

Now he was dead, probably because of Shelter.

How he knew that he could not have said. It was possible some cardplayers, not liking Sam Rutledge's bottom deal had killed him. Possible. But up here? Why up here, so far from town?

Sam had never been an outdoor man. He wouldn't have been riding to Massacre since ghosts are notoriously reluctant card players. Nor did they use hair restorer.

Shell dropped the bottle and covered it with pine needles. Then he unslung his pack and with effort and loathing he pulled the loosely held together sack of bones from the tree.

He weighed nothing. *Only a bundle of rags.* That was what he had to tell himself. He slowly dug a grave, using a broken branch, thinking of the other graves he had dug in his time.

Reluctantly he went through Sam's pockets, finding a sack with three double-eagles in it. That was revealing—robbery had not been the motive.

Indians? Shelter doubted that. Sam still had his hair and he had the red silk cravat which would have appealed to an Indian immensely.

"Sorry, Sam," Morgan said, "it looks like I got you tangled up in something."

Perfunctorily he went through the rest of Sam's pockets, expecting nothing. He found two fresh decks of cards, a handkerchief, a silver watch inscribed "S.A.R.", a letter from a woman in Sioux City, very personal, and then, the note.

The paper was stuck together with moisture, yellowed. The ink which was a particularly vivid blue was running. Shell opened it up and was immediately disappointed.

"Shell," it read. "Watch yourself. The . . ."

That was all. Shelter turned it over, re-read it twice

68

and then sat holding the note, as if it could reveal more than was written there.

Sam simply hadn't had time. He had started to write a letter and been interrupted. Hastily he had jammed it into his coat.

Slowly Shelter buried Sam Rutledge as the rain slanted down and the thunder blared taps. All the while he was thinking.

What could Sam have had to say, what was there to warn him about? Rutledge knew Shelter had already received the letter warning him that Middlesex was here. Knowing Shelter, he knew that the man would enter Sutler's Flats with caution.

"Watch yourself. The . . ."

It gnawed at his brain. It meant nothing. Just a few hurried words of warning intended to let Shelter know that things had changed? That things were not as they seemed? Who knew? Only Sam Rutledge and he was now only a slowly decomposing pile of earth and litter. Only Sam knew and Shelter had no faith in his spirit communicating with him. Whatever it was Sam meant to warn him about, Shelter would not know until it was too late.

"Thanks for trying, Sam." Shelter looked again at the rough grave, shook his head and turned away, returning to the trail, carrying a few memories of the little gambler with him up the lonely mountain.

That's all we leave, he thought. A few memories and a small hump of earth. Best try to make those memories good ones for those who remain behind.

The sky darkened still more. The clouds were an unruly crowd pushed back from the mountains by a policing wind. Rain fell in iron sheets, driving against

Shelter's face and body with cold intensity.

Sundown laced the clouds with deep, angry purple, and lightning probed their mass with ghostly, white fingers. Shelter stopped abruptly.

He had come to the crest of the trail and now it veered away sharply, running down into the narrow valley below. He could make out the geometric shape of a building now. It was old, as gray as the skies, and part of the wall had been pirated for some other purpose.

Beyond that, along the stump-studded slope he saw a vaguely red structure and then the clouds drew across the valley and he saw no more.

The rain was lighter now, but the wind against his face was icy. He walked on, plodding through the mud of the road. Once he thought he heard a shrill, faint whistle far away and his head came up, but it was not repeated.

He nearly tripped over the broken plank on the road. Squinting at it he saw crudely painted, the legend, "Massacre."

He had taken three more steps before the rifle sang out and he felt searing pain flare up in his brain. Shell had time to slap reflexively at his skull, time to feel the warmth of his own blood against his palm, and then there was no more time as he toppled forward, falling face downward against the cold, muddy earth, his fingers clenching involuntarily, sending messages to his uncomprehending brain.

He was alive.

That was the first thought to pry itself free of the dark, pervading unconsciousness and take form in

70

his mind. He was alive.

The world was dark, but the rain had stopped. He had a brief, panicked notion that he was dead, buried with Sam Rutledge in the cold, cold earth, and that was why the rain no longer reached him.

He shook that aside angrily. No, by God, he was alive!

He tried to order his thoughts, with no immediate success. He was alive, or dead and thought he was alive.

Someone had shot him! That came to him through the murky haze of thought. Someone had shot him. He had touched the hot seep of blood, felt the agony explode in his skull, and then there had been nothing for a long while.

Damnit, Morgan, come out of it! With sheer will power he managed to clear his head slightly, managed to assess the situation.

He was lying sprawled on his face . . . against a plank floor! Not in the road. He was inside. Now an eye struggled to tear itself open. He peered through slitted eyelids and saw nothing but darkness. His fingers, probing the floor reassured him. He was inside, it was no trick of the mind.

Inside. How? Finding no answer he proceeded with his checklist. He moved the fingers of both hands, discovering thereby that he had both arms still. His legs were another matter—he was sure they were down there somewhere, but it seemed more trouble than it was worth just then to try moving them.

It was easier to sleep . . . easier. If he slept, he would die! His heart started racing as that thought took hold.

"Damnit, Morgan," some rational component in that badly shaken brain shouted, "it does not follow! Sleep, man. Sleep," and he did.

When he awoke it was no lighter, but his head was clearer. The pain was worse, however. Slowly he lifted a hand which seemed a part of someone else's body and moved it toward his head.

With some delicate probing he found that his head had been bandaged. A bullet had grooved itself alongside his ear, tearing the scalp open slick as a skinning knife, but there seemed to be no real damage.

Bandaged. That slowly took on a vital importance. Someone had bandaged him and brought him to this place. But who was there?

For that matter where was he? Massacre, he assumed, but he couldn't even be sure of that.

Now Shelter could hear a burst of rain against the roof of the building where he lay. So it was still storming across the mountains. There was something he had to do . . . an idea was trying to form itself in the dark corner of his mind. Something . . . D.D.!

He sat up, his head filling with skyrockets. Then he toppled over again and lay there panting. D.D. had been snatched by someone. A helpless, friendless girl with death hanging over her.

"And you did a great job of taking care of her, Morgan," he told himself with anger. "Took her from under your nose."

All right. There was no sense in going on about it. Get up and make amends. Find that girl.

That was easier thought than accomplished. By

bracing himself on one stiff arm he was able to rise again to a seated posture, but it was precarious. He was going no farther and he knew it.

Slowly he sagged back, letting hope fade away, letting his weary body settle against the cold plank floor of this shack while the rain outside drummed on, while deep sleep drove away thoughts of D.D.

It was still when he came around again. He listened, his head flat against the floor of the building, one eye peering into the darkness. It was silent—the rain had stopped.

Now, as his eyes wandered, he saw a pencil thin band of sunlight leaking through the wall. Shelter watched it for a long while, watched as it crept across the flooring, revealing the rough sawn planks in tiny increments.

It was a long while before he realized there was a bundle in front of him, something which had not been there before.

A slow, crablike hand stretched out toward the bundle and unwrapped it. Food—someone had left something to eat. He couldn't have cared less. The smell of it knotted his stomach.

But it was time to get up. He had to get up, had to find the strength to rise, to live. Thrusting both hands out before him, he shoved and raised his chest. Scooting to a sitting position he rested, head hung, breath coming raggedly. After long minutes, with supreme effort, he made it to his feet, staggering immediately.

He put out an arm and found the wall of the place. He stood there breathing deeply, letting the dizziness go away. Slowly it passed and he began to circle the room, still leaning against the walls.

The door—he had found it, its upper edged limned with pale sunlight. Shell's hand ran down the rough planks until he found the knob which was cool, greasy and oval.

He turned it expectantly. Nothing. The door was locked. He yanked on it again with the same negative result.

"Hey! Hey out there, open up!" He shouted and his voice came out in a croak. He rattled the knob again, but it was useless.

"Damn it! Open up!"

Nothing. There was no response at all. But perhaps there was no one there. Someone could have found him, tucked him away and ridden for a doctor. Somehow he didn't believe that.

His legs were trembling now; his stomach was bunched up, fiery, tilted slightly sideways.

"They'll be back then," he told himself. He hadn't the strength to force the door, and he knew it. Instead he settled back onto the floor, examining the food parcel a little more closely now. Sourdough bread, beef jerky and a jar of water. There was nothing appetizing about it, but he knew he had to provide nourishment for his body and so he sat gnawing on the food, deciding that the jerky was venison and not beef.

He had simply to eat and rest. After a time someone would come and let him out. They didn't mean to kill him—the bandage and the food made that obvious. So he would simply wait.

His thoughts, simple and repetitive circled his brain. He fell asleep with his meal half finished, descending into an unhappy dreamland where he rode with Dinkum and a headless Jeb Thornton into a clearing where a hundred grinning James Middlesexes waited. He could see D.D. sprawled upon the ground, and when Middlesex smiled Shell saw that his teeth were made of gold eagles.

He awoke at dusk, feeling worse, but much stronger.

He rose without much trouble, his head banging away. Creeping to the small hole in the tarpaper which had allowed the sun to bleed through into the shack's interior, he saw a line of purple, glistening mountains outside.

Nightfall again and no one had come. He had taken enough of this, he decided. He would try the door again.

He bent low and examined the knob, determining that it was nonfunctional. There was no lock at all, but there was a bar outside—he could just make out the outline of a section of two by eight. That wouldn't give easily.

Prowling the shack again, he found a high window, boarded up now. That was more like it. There was only one pane of glass surviving in a window frame made for four twelve by twelve panes and Shelter, shoving out against the boards which covered the window, had the satisfaction of hearing rusted nails pry free.

Bracing himself better he struck at the plank with the heel of his hand and it sprung free on one end. The other end followed moments later. Cool air rushed into the shack and he could see now a grassy, dusk shadowed meadow, a hillside littered with tree

75

stumps, the purpling sky, gradually clearing above.

He went to work on the second plank which offered no more resistance than the first. Two more boards had to be knocked free and then, finding the window swollen into its frame, he smashed out the window and with a great deal of effort boosted himself up and over the sill.

He fell heavily to the ground outside, and angered with himself he rose and hobbled off. He had taken four steps when the voice called out.

"Hold it or I'll shoot you again."

And she meant it. Shelter stopped, sighing with frustration.

The girl in the outsized mackinaw, floppy hat and knee boots carried a big Sharps rifle across her forearm. "Is that what you tagged me with the first time?" Shelter asked as she took a step forward from out of the shadows.

"It is. I was just going to clip your ear off but you kinder turned your head." She was small—she would never see five feet, and had a deep voice which cracked from time to time, leaping an octave or so. The hatbrim shadowed her face and Shell could not make out her features. But he could smell her.

"Short on water up here?" he asked.

"What d'ya mean?" she asked.

"You smell like mule."

"And you smell like skunk to me. Don't forget who's got the gun, mister."

"I'm not likely to do that."

"I tried to be nice to you—left you food and bandaged you, but by God, I won't take insults!"

"Julie!" The voice came from around the corner

of the shack. "What's all the ruckus . . . oh!"

"He climbed out, Pa. Now what'll we do with him?"

The man was small, wiry, even dirtier than his daughter, and wore a streaked gray beard. He crept nearer to Morgan, eyeing him by the dim light of dusk.

"You don't leave us a lot of choice, mister," the man said.

"Now wait a minute!" Shell's anger was rising. "Your daughter shoots me, you drag me down here and lock me up. When I want to leave you say I've given you no choice. I don't know what your problem is, and I don't want to know. I just want to be left alone to leave. There's a girl in trouble out there who needs me."

"He means the Short bitch, Pa," Julie said.

"How in . . ."

"Don't use such language, girl," the old man said.

They seemed to know an awful lot about Shell's business. He looked at them singly, wondering . . . then it came to him. "You're Jack Shandy."

"As if you didn't know," Shandy said.

"He knew. He was with the Short . . . girl," Julie said, finding a new word to describe D.D. at her father's sharp glance.

"Come along," Shandy said after a while. "Julie you get behind him with that .50 and keep him honest."

"I will, Pa," the girl promised with icy tones.

"You come along, young fellah," Shandy said. He himself set off in an elbow swinging, hunched gait. Shelter glanced over his shoulder, saw the girl eagerly pointing the big Sharps at him and he followed.

Rounding the corner of the shack Shell could see what remained of Massacre. Down in the bottom of the muddy valley a dirty creek rushed past hillslopes littered with gray, tilted shacks.

Far away he could see three or four lights burning in other structures. Shandy turned, waved a hand and Shelter followed him up a badly rutted muddy road toward a low, dark building where the smoky light of a candle illuminated a single, oilcloth covered window.

Shandy, preceding them by a hundred feet went up to the shack, wiped his muddy boots on the lip of the sagging stoop, and opened the door.

Shelter, prodded now and then by the Sharps buffalo gun, followed him.

The interior of the shack was dingy, ragged but clean. Two puncheon chairs stood against the walls, a rag rug spattered color against a gray floor. An ancient musket and powder horn hung above a native stone fireplace.

There was a smaller room beyond, the scent of chickory and coffee hung in the air along with another, more acidic scent which might have been mustard greens.

Jack Shandy had removed his weathered hat and now, by the light of the candle, Shelter could see that he was tattered, weary and even older than he had believed.

The girl, leaving her hat on, perched on the table, rifle following Shelter.

"Set," Shandy ordered, nodding toward one of

the roughly hewn chairs and Shelter did so.

"I want an explanation," Morgan said.

"You want one!" Julie laughed. Her voice broke into a squeak.

"Hush, Julie." The old man lit a handmade pipe and puffed at it thoughtfully for a moment. "The way I see it we got us a problem here, Mister . . ."

"Shelter Morgan," the tall man provided. His eyes were cold, Shandy noticed, maybe the coldest eyes he had ever seen and Jack Shandy in his fifty years in the wilderness had seen some.

"The way I see it is we got us a problem," Shandy began again. He took the chair beside Shelter and looked at him closely for a minute.

"Shoot him," Julie suggested, "that'll eliminate the problem right quick."

"Well, we might just have to do that," Shandy said with little regret. "But we'll let the man make his choice."

"A choice," Shell repeated. Were they both mad? Short had thought Shandy was and Morgan could believe it. The way those little eyes glittered, the way his narrow chin dropped in a soundless, toothless laugh. His next statement convinced Shelter beyond any doubt.

"Yes, sir, Mister Shelter Morgan. I b'lieve I'll let you choose. You can either spend the next five years in Massacre's jail . . . or you can become our next town marshal."

6.

Shelter could only sit and stare at the hollow cheeked old man before him. What had he walked into? And what a time for it, with D.D. gone and Middlesex due to return from Tucson—if he was not already back. And now this fool of an old man was offering him either prison or a badge.

The girl sat like a lump on the table, the gun muzzle never wavering.

"Well?" Shandy snapped.

"I don't understand any of this," Shell said honestly. "Why lock me up anyway? Why try to kidnap a man to make him town marshal? Either way it makes no damn sense to me."

"I don't like strong talk," Shandy chided softly.

"What I don't like," Shell exploded, "is being shot at, jailed and striking deals with madmen!"

"Don't you say that about Pa," Julie squeaked. Shelter only glowered at her.

Then she removed her hat and Shell practically fell out of his chair. She had the features of a doll. Wide blue eyes, dark glossy hair which cascaded free as she removed her hat, ripe, strawberry mouth, pale complexion—all ruined by streaks of dirt.

"Suppose you tell me exactly what this is about," Shelter asked. "Then I'll tell you why I have to go. There's a girl alone out there in a great deal of danger. You must understand that . . ."

"Oh, I understand more than you think, Morgan," Shandy growled. Then he rose stiffly and retrieved a jug of whisky from a badly hung wall cabinet.

"I don't care for any," Shelter said.

"I think you'd better have some," Shandy insisted, taking two grimy tin cups from the shelf. "Look at it this way—it's either a gesture of kindness to a condemned man—that's you, or a toast to my pact with the new town marshal . . . also you," Shandy said. "You see," he handed a tincup full of white corn liquor to Shell, "it's all up to you, Morgan. Me, I'm flexible in such matters."

Shell took a drink of the whisky only to wash away some of the red anger he felt building. He was dealing with a madman.

The whisky burned his throat and settled into his stomach uncomfortably.

"Suppose you lay this all out for me," Shell requested.

"You understand me."

"Let's suppose I don't—a condemned man's last request: lay it out for me nice and plain, Shandy."

"All right." Shandy leaned back in his chair, his eyes glittering oddly. "Let's see—do you know what's happening in these hills?"

"Let's say I don't know anything," Shell answered.

"All right. I'll keep it simple. Me and a man named Ken Short found gold up in these hills years back. We built us a town—you was lookin' at it. We named it Massacre after a bunch of Irish boys who got killed working for us.

"Now," Shandy took a long pull of whisky and refilled his glass from the jug at his feet. "We ran into some lean times up here, Morgan. Vein played out. Had us two hard winters and the shafts got flooded. Indians hit us two, three times."

"But you kept going," Shell remarked. The old man nodded. Shelter noticed that Julie Shandy had shed her mackinaw and he noticed that she had been concealing a lot worth seeing underneath it.

"To continue," Shandy said, his eyes flickering from Shelter to Julie. "Times got tough. I could see we was going to have to plow some of what we took out back into the mines to develop them properly. My partner, Ken Short, he didn't have the stomach for that. He figured he had gotten the cream and he wanted to keep what he had, so we parted ways. Not real friendly-like, but anyway . . .

"With what I had I kept working. Massacre started to wither on the vine. Wasn't no miners, wasn't nothing to keep gold flowing into the saloons—oh, they had 'em—never liked having saloons in town, but they had 'em. Should've passed an ordinance. I was mayor, you know. Still am."

"Not much to be mayor of anymore, is it?" Shelter asked.

"No. Three weeks ago there was only three of us

living in Massacre. Now," he added, scratching his whiskered chin, "I suppose she'll build up again. It's inevitable."

"Do you mean you've made a new strike?"

"Oh, sure. Twice as rich as before. I always knew it was down there, of course. I always could read rock. Then," he sighed, "the word got out. Somehow it got out. I guess my first shipment to Tucson got them all buzzing. So the trouble started up."

"What kind of trouble?"

"By God! As if you didn't know," Julie said angrily, hopping down from the table. "Pa, this is getting plumb ridiculous, telling him everything he already knows."

"Settle down, girl," Shandy said. "More whisky?" Shelter shook his head. "What happened of course is that the vultures started roosting in Massacre. Taking up residence, you might say, in the old hotels, the old mine barracks. Hell, I can't work my mine now. They'd just skim off all the ore I brought up—and you may have noticed, there ain't no law for a long ways out here, sonny."

"I've noticed."

Julie gave him an "I'll bet you have" look, and shifted her rifle.

"One of these men, he volunteered some information. Told us that there was a man named Middlesex behind this. Middlesex, as I suppose you don't know is the son-in-law of Ken Short. The man's got claim to half my diggings! It ain't right, but it's the law. Him and old Ken's daughter mean to take their half. You see," Shandy took another drink. His face was flushed with whisky now, his eyes brighter than ever, "if Middlesex and that girl take my ore I can't complain to anybody—half of what I got is theirs, no matter that it's my money and labor that brought it to the surface."

"You never terminated the contract you had with Ken Short."

"Naw," Shandy waved a hand. "Short was lily livered and stubborn as a jack mule, but he would never have touched an ounce of this gold. He was a proud man. Middlesex, now, he's a polecat."

"He knows that, Pa," Julie interrupted with impatience. "He should, he works for him, don't he?"

"Do I?" Shell asked, amused at the thought.

"Leastwise that's what we figure," Shandy said. "You was seen with the girl, riding this way. You come into Massacre. So Julie shot at you, just to scare you off—missed a little, didn't you girl? Told you not to cut it so fine."

"Yes, Pa," the girl, obviously abashed, answered.

"That's how it stands, Morgan. Now then," he leaned back, clasping a knee. "Of course you'd deny it all—any man on the spot would. So it come to me to give you a choice, to prove your intentions, your guilt or innocence, as it may be. You take my offer, become Massacre's town marshal, run out all of them buzzards who are squatting on my property—or go to jail. For about five years, I'd say."

"Shandy," Shell said with a slow exhalation, "you can go to hell. I don't like you, your town or your choices."

"Told you he'd say that," Julie offered.

"Yes, yes you did." Shandy smiled. "Now that

could be a good sign or a bad sign. Could be Mister Morgan is a dyed-in-the-wool Middlesex man or it could be he's a tough hombre not given to bein' railroaded."

"Look, Shandy. . . !" Shell's patience was gone.

"Hush now," the old man said. "We got something that'll persuade you. Persuade you if you are a Middlesex man or persuade you if you are what you claim—just a man on a white horse trying to protect a fair maiden."

"The hell you do," Morgan snapped. He was ready to stand, make a try for the rifle, as weak as he felt it beat the other alternatives: five years in some shack or deserting D.D. to play lawman for an addled old man. He was about to make his move . . . and then the door to the inner room opened and he saw her.

"D.D.!"

It was D.D., looking weary and disheveled and Shelter started to rise. Two things stopped him: the rifle which Julie jabbed at him and the sight of the big Indian behind D.D.

He was huge for an Indian, a long nosed, long jawed scowling man with blue-black hair falling straight across his shoulders. He had a slightly closed eye which was surrounded by a yellowish-purple bruise.

"I tagged him once good," Shelter thought with hollow satisfaction.

"Shell . . ." D.D. tried to come to him, but the Indian wrapped a massive, mahogany forearm around her throat and held her back.

"You see . . ." Shandy was positively jovial. Shell

could have strangled him. "If you're a Middlesex man you don't want her hurt, do you? If you're only a friend, well I guess you feel the same."

That told Shelter something—Shandy didn't realize that Middlesex would like nothing better than to see D.D. dead. The mining claim would then become his property. He said nothing.

Watching Shandy he wondered how far the man would go, how crazy he actually was. One thing was obvious, with a sort of relief tempered by uncertainty Shell considered that he did not have to worry about D.D. wandering through the wilderness, about her being killed by Middlesex.

"You'll let her go if I do what you want?" he asked.

"Why, shore!" Shandy agreed expansively. Shelter trusted him not a bit, but it was the best deal he was going to get out of this.

"I'll be marshal of Massacre."

"Fine, fine." Shandy slapped his knee as if they were great friends. "I'll swear you in and get you a badge."

"And a gun," Morgan said as Shandy made to rise.

"Now that is one thing I'm regretful about, sonny. I can't let you have a gun. You see that."

"Then how in hell am I going to run off those hardcases?" Shell demanded.

"I don't rightly know." Shandy scratched his head. "But I guess you lawmen got your ways."

Shell laughed out loud despite himself. Shandy turned in surprise, Julie frowned angrily. D.D. looked as if she would faint. The Indian stood immobile as stone.

"Take her out of here now, Casco," Shandy said, speaking to the Indian.

The man nodded and backed from the room, his black eyes unreadable. Shandy had returned and he took a small object from his pocket, tossing it to Shelter who caught it reflexively. It was a tin star, tarnished and crudely made. "Marshal" was all it said.

"Now I guess we got to swear you in, Mister Morgan. Does an oath mean anything to you?"

"It does, under most circumstances," Shell said dryly.

"Well, anyway. Stand up if you would."

Julie shifted to the corner of the room, her rifle never wavering. "You can put it away now, Julie. I think Mister Morgan understands me. Casco, he ain't got the morals of a white man—never read the Bible. But he's loyal as he can be to me. I've told him."

Shelter looked a question at Shandy.

"I've told him to kill the girl if Mister Morgan tried to release her or went back on this sacred oath he's about to swear. Now, Mister Morgan, let's get on with it. Raise your right hand, please."

Shandy recited some meaningless words, pausing for Shell to repeat them. Julie stood in the corner, her eyes defiant, seemingly unashamed of any of this high handedness. Morgan glanced once toward the inner room. The door was closed, likely barred, and behind it Casco sat watching D.D., waiting for an excuse to kill her.

When Shandy was through, Shell looked at the

badge in his hand, shook his head and pinned it on, first rubbing it on his sleeve to shine it up a little.

"There now," Shandy said to his daugher with obvious satisfaction, "I told you everything would work out all right. We got us a new marshal and he's going to clean up Massacre properly."

7.

The new town marshal of Massacre stood in the cold starlight outside the Shandy house, looking down the dark, high ridged valley toward the ghost town itself. Run-off water sparkled on the slopes of the hills and far below yellow lanternlight shone in the windows of two of the reclaimed buildings.

He started on down—what else was there to do? D.D. was in their hands, and they appeared to have no more compunctions about killing her than her husband did. In the back of his mind was the thought that he could take someone's gun, return to the house and force them to release D.D. On serious consideration, however, that seemed more hazardous to D.D.'s safety than carrying out Shandy's improbable plan.

Run them out. Just walk up to two dozen hired fighting men and ask them to leave. Tap the badge on the shirt front, that ought to scare them out of these hills.

Shelter halted beside the shed where he had been

held prisoner. No sense walking right down the main road. There would likely be a guard somewhere.

He climbed the denuded slope behind the shed and crept along the muddy, rough hillside in the darkness until he was above the town.

Looking down into the dark, shadowed canyon he could see no movement. Now and then a voice was raised, however, from a long, gray building which perched precariously on the slate littered slope. That, probably, was the old miners' barracks.

Above and beyond that Shelter could just make out two upright timbers and a massive cross beam set into the hillside. The entrance to the Shandy mine.

Six or seven buildings in great disrepair lay scattered along a winding muddy road. Some of them had been savaged for fire wood, others the weather had mauled. Heavy snows had swayed the roofs of the poorly, hastily constructed boom town shacks.

Shelter sat on the cold hillside, the wind whistling past him, sizing up the barracks and the building across from it—a makeshift saloon, he decided, by the activity, the shouting.

The barracks itself had a side door, two back windows, two black iron chimneys, one of them sending spirals of white smoke against the dark sky. The saloon, if that was what it was, had no side door that Shelter could see, but the building was nearly identical to the barracks, and if it had been built to the same plan, there would be a door on the north side, toward the mine.

He waited for nearly an hour, watching for his chance. And then it came. A single man staggered out of the saloon's front door and walked through the ankle deep mud to the alley which ran beside the building.

Shelter slipped down the hill, through the jagged stumps and rotting timber, arriving breathless and panting at the road below. He moved into the shadows of the empty buildings and crept up the alley, his eyes searching the darkness. There should have been guards posted, but then again perhaps they didn't expect anyone foolish enough to try attacking their fortress single-handedly.

Shelter eased up to the corner of the building, flinching as a rat scuttled away in the darkness. Peering around the corner he saw his man. He was a bulky, big shouldered man who just now leaned up against the side of the building, supporting himself with one hand while he raised a cloud of steam.

Shelter stepped out and was behind him with three quick steps. Shell cocked his fist and brought it around with all of his weight behind it. It caught the outlaw where he intended it to, on the neck just below and behind the ear and the man went face downward into the cold mud, a single, surprised grunt escaping.

Shell crouched low, quickly stripped the gunbelt from the outlaw, found a knife and took that as well. Then he retreated to the alley, walking swiftly past the saloon, ducking under a back window.

All right, you've got a gun. What now?

Now if you simply wave a pistol at them these bad men will be frightened and go away. Sure they would, after they had tromped Shelter into the mud.

He crouched against the building for a while, the thought returning that he should try to take D.D.

and get the hell out of here. The memory of Casco's black, lifeless eyes came back to him vividly. He had D.D. in that windowless back room, and he was willing and able to kill her apparently, out of some misplaced loyalty to the old man.

"Damnit, Morgan. One day you're going to have to sit down and figure out how you get into these things."

Right now it was time to figure a way *out* of it.

That man in the alley wouldn't stay unconscious forever, it was time to move now. Shelter eased toward the street, and looking up and down, crossed it, walking casually. Once across he eased behind the building, tucked his pistol into his belt and looked up.

Placing a foot on the window sill he managed to stretch up, catch the edge of the roof, throw a knee up and roll onto the canted roof.

Walking silently across the roof he came to the iron chimney. Smoke spewed out into the night sky and Shelter turned his face away from the smoke and cinders, inching toward it. Taking off his shirt he balled it up, ripped back the rusted conical canopy and jammed his shirt down into the stove pipe.

Moving swiftly but quietly back to the edge of the roof he swung down to the muddy earth. Shivering with the cold he raced around the building, past another rickety shack. Then he moved back toward the street.

He was just in time to see the first man come rushing out of the barracks. He was wearing long johns and was bootless. His choking could be heard all the way up the street.

A second man followed, yelling and cussing.

"The barracks is on fire!"

It wasn't, but smoke now rolled out the door in billowing clouds, and it gave a good imitation of a building on fire. Now the door to the saloon opened and a lanternlit outlaw appeared.

"What in the hell. . . !" he ducked back inside and Shelter, crouched in the darkness, heard his muffled shouts. In minutes the street was crowded with men rushing from the saloon toward the baracks where all of their worldly possessions were stored.

With all eyes on the barracks—someone had tried to start a bucket brigade although no flames were visible, a fact that had yet to sink in—Shelter crossed the street again, went to the saloon's side door and entered. The building was empty.

Shell quickly crossed the sawdust strewn floor of the ratty saloon, found a coal oil lantern and smashed it against the floor. Liquid fire bled out across the floor and licked at the rough, jerry-built bar.

Glancing at the doorway Shelter backed to the far wall, found another lantern, and after splashing coal oil on the wall and floor, touched it off with the still burning lantern.

Quickly he backed from the saloon, going out through the side door into the dark alley. Already the flames had caught and were greedily devouring the saloon.

From the street a cry went up.

"The saloon! The saloon's on fire!"

Shelter turned and ran in a half-crouch up the

alley, catching the orange-red glow of flames from the corner of his eyes. He rounded the corner of the alley and came face to face with a man.

Morgan pulled up sharply, caught off guard. His opponent was set, waiting however, and before Shell could react he swung out with a jarring right hook which caught Shell flush on the jaw and sent him sprawling.

Shelter could see eyes and teeth gleaming dully in the firelight and then the man moved in, reaching for a gun beneath the heavy coat he wore.

Shell whipped out with his legs, taking the man from his feet. He landed with a thud and both men struggled to their feet. Shelter saw his own pistol lying in the mud, but it had landed too far away to do him any good.

As the outlaw reached again for his belt gun, Shelter lunged at him, gripping his right wrist, bringing up a knee which glanced off the outlaw's thigh.

Together they toppled to the earth, landing with a splat. The outlaw struck out viciously. A right grazed Shell's temple, a left hand clawed at his eyes. Shelter buried his face against the hollow of the man's shoulder and slammed three tremendous right hooks into the body, hearing the muffled crack of a rib.

Enraged the outlaw rolled, throwing Shelter aside. He was a big man and he towered over Shell, his hair hanging across his face. The fire roared now and the alley was as light as day. The two men circled each other.

Shelter feinted with a left and tried an overhand right, but the outlaw had done some fighting. He blocked it neatly, countered with his own whistling

94

right which caught Shell on the chest, and moved in.

Shell felt the whirring begin in his skull and he fought it off. The big outlaw was against him, wrapping mammoth arms around his chest, trying to squeeze the life from him. He lifted Shelter from the ground and grunted with the exertion as he tried to crush his ribcage.

Shell jammed the heel of his hand against the outlaw's nose, but the man shrugged it off. Shelter felt the world start to tumble and spin, to slide away as his lungs fought for breath. The steely grip of the big man never faltered.

Shell suddenly brought his head down hard, butting the outlaw across the bridge of his nose. Blood splattered both men and the outlaw fell back with a yowl of pain, holding his broken nose.

Shelter followed him back, hammering with lefts and rights. He had the man backed up against the building now and he slammed blow after blow against the outlaw.

Still the man fought back, covering up well, and Shelter began to feel a rising panic. The fire was burning brightly still. All it needed was for one man to enter the alleyway, size up the fight and take Shelter down.

With a mounting fury Shell continued to hammer at the big man, taking a stiff punch now and then for his troubles.

The outlaw was faltering. Shell could feel it now. A tremendous shot to the wind took much of the life out of the big man, and Shelter saw him sag against the wall, his hands in front of his face, pawing out at Shelter.

Then suddenly there was an opening. The smallest of opportunities; a split second reaction brought Shelter's high hard left hook up and over the sagging guard of the outlaw and his knuckles collided with the exposed cheekbone of the big man.

His lights went out. The big man's eyes rolled back, showing only white and he slid slowly down the wall, only a huge, inert sack of potatoes.

Shelter stepped back panting, his heart racing. His chest was filled with fiery pain and simultaneously he was shivering violently with the cold.

He staggered to where his gun lay, plucked it from the mud and then, hearing approaching voices, he dove for the cover of an abandoned mine wagon which lay loaded with refuse at the end of the alley.

"Now what the hell?" he heard someone say.

"It's Red."

"What the hell happened."

"Another fight. Come on. Let's get him the hell out of here before the building falls on him."

Shell could see the two firelit men bend over and drag Red from the alley. He heard their grunts and curses, heard one of them mumble, "It's going to be a damned cold winter without that whisky."

"What do you think happened. . . ?"

Their voices faded out and Shell rose from behind the wagon, and holding his side with his left hand he stumbled from the alley and up the hillslope into the cover of darkness.

The sky was iron gray. Smoke wafted into the night sky, the crimson, jutting flames stood like a beacon above the ghost town.

Shelter staggered across the hillside, falling a

dozen times in the mud.

He knew that he had done as much as he could do, he also knew that it was not nearly enough. The Middlesex men would be inconvenienced, but they would not leave.

He approached the Shandy house, his teeth chattering, his body battered, feet caked with mud. He happened to glance toward the slope behind the house and he saw her there—Julia Shandy with that murderous Sharps rifle. She watched him go up to the house but she made no gesture, said nothing.

The door was locked and he had to pound on it before Shandy lifted the bar and let Shell into the smoky, dingy room.

"Didn't hear no shooting," was the first thing he said.

"Get me something to dry off on."

"I didn't hear no shooting," Shandy repeated.

"That's because there wasn't any!" Shell said angrily. He wrapped his arms around his shoulders and went nearer to the fireplace where a few dully glowing coals gave off a minimum of heat.

Shandy had produced a clean, frayed towel and he gave it to Shell. The old man sat in his rocker, eyeing Shelter with suspicion.

"Should've been shooting. What's the matter, couldn't you bring yourself to shoot your friends?"

"They're not my friends."

"How come I didn't hear no shooting then?"

"Probably because you sent me down there without a gun," Shelter answered. He was in a smoldering mood. He dried his arms and chest roughly.

"You got a gun now," Shandy said, nodding at the mud-caked Colt thrust into Shell's belt.

"Look—I just didn't use the gun. God's sake, Shandy, look out the window, why don't you!"

Shandy did so, grunting with animal satisfaction. The fire reddened the sky for miles. "You do that?" he asked suspiciously, turning toward Shelter again.

"Yes."

"I owned that building," Shandy said.

Shelter muttered a disgusted curse, slapped the muddy, useless pistol on the table, sat down and drew off his boots.

"You didn't do much," Shandy said.

"I did what I could."

"Thought you'd be a better marshal," Shandy said with what seemed to be genuine regret. Shelter stared at him with astonishment. *Mad.* The man was truly mad.

"I imagine it took Hickok more than a night to clean up Abilene," Shelter said. He looked around, pulled a chair up to the fire and sagged into it wearily.

"Rome wasn't built in a day, and all that?" Shandy said. Shelter didn't bother to answer him.

After a long silent minute, he warned the miner: "Look, they may figure you set that fire. They're liable to come storming up here."

"Not likely," Shandy winked. "Don't you think they've tried that? They know about Julie and that Sharps rifle of hers. They know she can shoot the whiskers off a gnat. There's two men buried beside that road, men who tried to come up to this house. No sir, they won't try it."

"Listen, Shandy," Shell said leaning forward, hands clasped together, "doesn't tonight prove I'm not with Middlesex? Why don't you let me take the girl and ride out of here? Damnit, man, I'm no friend of James Middlesex. I want him, probably worse than you do."

"So you say," Shandy grunted. He had his pipe out and now he stuffed the bowl and lit it.

"It's true, Shandy."

"Is it? Why, then? Why do you want Middlesex?"

Slowly Shelter told the story, a story he had told a hundred times, a story which never failed to bring the bloody memories to life. He spoke in a soft voice and Shandy listened closely, puffing on his stubby pipe.

When Shelter was through the old man simply said, "Sounds like somethin' Middlesex would be involved in."

"So you see . . ."

"I don't see nothin'! It don't take much to concoct a story like that. No, sir. We made us a bargain, Mister Shelter Morgan. You clean those vultures out of Massacre if you want this Middlesex woman back."

"All right." Shelter was too tired to argue. He had taken a beating in Sutler's Flats, walked a good many miles in bad weather, been shot, and tonight's episode had finished sapping his strength. Perhaps in the morning his thoughts would be clearer, maybe he could come up with some way to budge this old man's iron resolve. Just now it was all he could do to keep his head up.

"I've got to sleep, Shandy."

"All right," he drawled, "though I don't know what you're tired from—you didn't even shoot nobody."

Shelter was too weary to respond. He was led through the front door where he could still see the flames against the sky, and out around the house. Passing through a grove of young aspen they came to a squat shack.

"In here," Shandy said. He took a lantern down, lit it and showed Shelter the room.

A low bed covered with an Indian blanket stood against one wall, a dollhouse sized table and chair against the other. There was no stove, no fireplace, but the walls kept the wind out. It would do.

"I'll come for you in the morning," Shandy said. "You can eat and then I'll expect you to get down into Massacre and shoot some of them men."

Shelter didn't have the strength to smile. The situation was absurd, but not funny. Shandy went out, pulling the door shut and with distant disgust Shelter heard a bar of some sort dropped, and he knew Shandy had locked him in.

It didn't seem to matter just them. He stood, turned out the lantern and then kicked off his boots. Sitting on the side of the bed he hung his head for a moment, his mind blank. Then, rousing himself, he pulled off his pants and slipped into the bed which was as hard as rocks.

That didn't matter either. He drew the Indian blanket up to his ears and he was warm. The hell with it all . . . he yawned . . . tomorrow his mind would be clearer and he could handle this. Just now he would sleep, just sleep.

What time it was when he heard the sound he did not know. He knew he must have been asleep for several hours, knew that it was dark and still outside. He knew that someone had entered the shack, and that was all he did know.

Until he felt the blanket drawn back momentarily, felt the bed shift as added weight was placed upon it, felt the warm brush of feminine flesh against his thigh and chest, felt the warm, pliant lips of Julie Shandy meet his own.

8.

Julie was against him in the night and he was aware of the firm energy of her young muscles, of the swelling of her abundant breasts, of the silky touch of her hair. Her hands, lithe and capable moved across his chest, gripped his shoulders and she pressed herself against him. She had bathed at least. She smelled of lye soap and of young girls.

Shell did not respond at all and she noticed it. She drew back, smiling.

"What's the matter, Shelter?"

"The matter," he repeated sleepily. "Nothing at all the matter with me."

There was a moment's cold silence. "Are you angry with me still."

"Just for shooting me?" he asked with mock astonishment. "Of course not. Did you bring your gun with you tonight, in case I was uncooperative."

"I don't like your attitude," she said, sulking.

"I'm not crazy about yours, Julie. What is this, anyway, some plan to gain leverage over me."

"A plan!" she seemed genuinely outraged this time.

She hovered over him and Shelter could sense rather than see the pendulous weight of those ripe young breasts, the dark indignation on her face, the heat of her thigh which still pressed against his, the slope and hump of her firm buttocks.

She was a hell of a good looking girl, and apparently an eager one, but it's hard to make love to a woman who holds a gun to your head.

"I came on my own." Her voice was softer now, the anger fading. Her words were blurred by sensuality as she leaned forward once again and Shelter felt the soft, warm pressure of her breasts against his chest, felt the small hand against his thigh.

"What's the matter? Don't be like that, Shelter, don't hold a grudge."

He managed not to laugh out loud. Her lips met his gently, tasting one corner of his mouth and then the other before they parted and like the soft, dewy petals of a flower encompassed his lips.

"Don't you like me at all?"

"We've just met," he said.

"And you want me to go?" she asked petulantly. Suddenly he wasn't so sure of that.

Her hair was draped across his chest, soft, warm, sweet smelling.

"Can't I convince you I'm a friend? I didn't know at first, you see? I shot to warn you away. I hurt you but I didn't mean to. I still thought you were one of them, of course, but then I heard you talk to Pa. He doesn't believe you, but I do now."

"Do you?"

"Of course." She kissed each ear, her breasts swaying across his chest tantalizingly as she moved from side to side. "Don't you believe me?" she asked as a child might. She kissed his bare shoulder and her hand tightened on his thigh. He felt her throw her leg up and over his, felt the soft brush of her crotch against the muscles of his thigh as she did so.

The girl had some convincing arguments, there was no doubt about that. He was starting to believe her. To believe her with a rush of blood and a slow swelling, a responsive quickening of his pulse.

He placed an arm around her softly molded shoulders and she sighed with gratification, letting herself go slack against him. They were pressed together, thigh and abdomen, breast and lips.

Julie's hand reached down between her own legs and she found Shelter's growing erection. She fondled it gently, experimentally, her fingers light as they ran along the length of the shaft to the head, and Shell, looking up at her in the darkness, saw that her eyes were bright, her lips parted.

"You're not mad anymore," she whispered, taking a tiny bite of his ear lobe.

"Not just now."

"I'll apologize," she promised. "I'll apologize in a nice way. Very nicely."

As she spoke her hand continued to work against Shell's cock, bringing it to full life, to pulsing readiness. Now he could feel the damp warmth of her crotch, feel Julie's fingers, his erection tangled up in stroking sensuality.

She pressed her mouth against his hard, and lifting herself slightly, she inserted the very tip of his shaft.

The touch was warm, nearly agonizing in its pleasurability, but Shelter held back, forced himself to keep from arching his back, thrusting out with his pelvis, driving it into her, burying himself in her warmth.

She murmured syllables of no meaning into his ear and he felt her body tauten. She buried her face against his chest, lavishing kisses on shoulders, throat and chest. Her hips twitched slightly, like some great, pagan engine just coming to life and then with a shudder she lowered herself onto Shelter, a pleasured grunt coming to her lips as she writhed from side to side, settling herself.

"I'm sorry," she murmured. "I said I'd apologize and I do. I'm sorry, sorry." Her hand reached out behind her magnificent buttocks and cupped his sack, hefting it as if she would draw them into her as well.

Meanwhile her fluid hips had begun a slow sideways motion which electrified the head of Shell's erection and he thrust out once, drawing a pleased response from Julie.

His hands ran down her back, across the sleek, taut flesh of her to the rising mound of her buttocks. He clenched her tightly to him and his lips sought her breasts.

She arched her back so that his mouth could find those eager, dark nipples and she threw her head back, smiling in the darkness as his lips and teeth teased them. Her hips now worked methodically, thrusting and retreating, her legs slowly spreading, entreating him to split her, to dive inside of the dark, safe hollow of her body.

She collapsed against him and the methodical hips became a wild, driving animal force. Her pelvis hammered against his. Her fingers clawed at his shoulder. She fell against him, her head turning from side to side as she breathed out passionate, many-voweled words.

She was all fluid motion and need, driving energy and warm flesh as she crawled over him, her lips sucking, her thighs clasping, her tireless hips pounding at him, tearing at his body.

Shell could hold back no longer. He began to hammer back at her, to join the struggle, to finish the battle which no one could lose.

He gripped the soft halves of her buttocks tenaciously, and he found her rhythm, meeting each stroke of hers with a deep, hearty thrust and she gasped out loud.

They were a tangle of ripe, tumescent flesh, a two-backed beast in violent confrontation with itself, trying to become one saturated, empty entity.

Shelter felt Julie suddenly halt her motion, poise above him and then with a burst of mad ecstasy she writhed against him, pitching and rolling, madly grinding against him. A small cry escaped her lips and Shelter, feeling the irrepressible urge growing in his loins, the demanding pulsing need to complete the act, began to tear at her, to plunge into her, to fight back in this wild melee of passion.

He drove it deep once, twice. He held her to him and buried himself to the hilt and she gasped again and then she stopped. She sagged against him and Shelter felt her go soft inside, felt her begin to quiver and tremble and he penetrated deeply, holding himself like that, back arched, every muscle tense until he reached his own orgasm with a tremendous draining of his loins, with a drumming of his own blood in his ears, with the woman, soft, pliant clinging to him in the night, her soft sighs in his ears.

Shelter closed his eyes then, deeply satisfied, deeply exhausted. He closed his eyes for only a moment, it seemed, and when he opened them again she was gone. Daylight leaked into the shack through the loosely fitting planks.

Shell swung his feet to the floor, and rubbing his eyes, he walked naked across the room, feeling stiffness everywhere in his body.

When he tried the door he found that it was still barred. With a faint smile he shook his head, dressed in boots and pants and sagged back onto the bed, waiting.

It was still early, he discovered as the door opened and Jack Shandy, backlighted by an orange sunrise stepped in.

"Mornin', marshal," Shandy said. He had a shotgun in his hands. Now from across his forearm he took a clean dark blue shirt and tossed it to Shell.

"Thanks."

"Get into it and let's eat. Then you can get down into town and start shootin' some of those varmints."

Without replying Shell tugged the shirt on, finding it a hair tight, and buttoned it. Then, with Shandy stepping into the far corner to watch him, he went out the door into the crisp morning.

Water glistened on the trees, the hills were mirrored with run-off in the bright morning light. They traipsed through the damp grove of slender aspens and went up to the main house.

Stepping in he saw D.D. and the Indian standing behind her as she sat over an apparently untouched plate of food. He saw now that one ankle was tied to the puncheon chair and Shelter spun angrily to face Shandy.

"Damnit, Shandy, you don't have to keep her tied up like an animal!"

"I cain't lose her, Mister Morgan. If I lose her I figure I lose my marshal, and I need you."

The Indian, Casco, looked to Shandy for instructions, but Shandy just shook his head. "Mister Morgan won't give us any trouble, Casco, will you, Marshal?"

"Not now." Shelter's voice came from between tightly compressed lips. "Not just now, Jack Shandy. But I'm warning you, if anything happens to her . . ."

"You don't have to warn me. I guess you've made your feelings about her clear."

Shandy was looking toward the doorway to the back room and Shelter's eyes followed. He saw Julie standing there, her hair brushed out sleekly. She wore a yellow ribbon in her hair and a clean blouse. Her face was scrubbed, her cheeks stained pink.

She looked from Shelter to D.D. and back and then with expressive silence she walked by Morgan, taking her Sharps from behind the door. She went out and Shandy stood chuckling with delight.

"Set and eat, Marshal," the old man said, "set and eat!"

Shelter took a chair to the table, watching the Indian who had backed off a few steps. D.D. looked to him with plaintive eyes and as he seated himself her hand stretched out across the table and took his.

"What's happening, Shelter? God, what are they trying to do?"

"Don't worry about this, D.D. We're getting out soon." He smiled and she almost believed him. Shandy laughed derisively and walked away, shaking his head.

When he returned he carried a plate of ham and beans, biscuits and grits. "Fill yourself up, Marshal. No sense trying to work on an empty stomach."

"Marshal?" D.D. looked from Shelter to Shandy, her forehead corrugated with puzzlement. "What does he mean, Shelter? Why is he calling you marshal."

"It's one of Shandy's little jokes, D.D. Mister Shandy is full of them."

She sighed, not understanding but knowing she was going to learn nothing else. She also knew that her only chance for escape lay with the tall, blue-eyed man, and she could see that despite his deliberate casualness, he was worried every bit as much as she.

"The girl's through eatin', Casco," Shandy said suddenly, "take her away."

The Indian nodded and moved forward. D.D. looked pleadingly at Shelter, but there was nothing he could do. He had to look away, Shandy's maddening chuckle in his ears.

"You're a real bastard, Jack Shandy," Morgan said.

"Mebbe," Shandy agreed with surprising good

humor. "Mebbe I am. It's survival, though, sonny. It's all a battle for survival, isn't it? Me, I'm tryin' my best to survive in a world that's ganged up against me.

"Now then, when you're done, you get down there and start shootin' some men."

"I'm not going down." Shelter dropped his fork deliberately and it clattered against the table.

"We have an agreement, Mister Morgan," Shandy said and all of the good humor was suddenly gone.

"Not in the daylight," Shelter said. "I'm not walking down there and getting myself killed. It won't do either of us any good if you ask me to do that."

"You'll go tonight?" Shandy scratched his chin whiskers.

"I guess I have to, don't I? Yes, I'll go tonight. In the meantime, let me eat. After breakfast I want you to lay out the town for me. I want to know every inch of it. The mine included."

"The mine?" Shandy's eyebrows drew together in suspicious disapproval. "I can't see what the mine lay-out has got to do with your job."

"It may have something to do with it, it may have nothing to do with it. Anyway, I want to know my town." He smiled thinly. "I want to know more about it than those men down below. It may be the only way to survive."

They spent the day sketching the lay-out of the town on brown wrapping paper. Shelter asked probing questions from time to time, wanting to know where windows were located, how much crawlspace was under a certain building.

110

When they got to the mine diagram Shandy grew reluctant, but Shell prodded him on. Every shaft, stope and pit had to be drawn out and explained to Shelter's satisfaction. With these diagrams Shandy was incredibly accurate. He had dug most of the mine, inch by inch with his own two hands and he knew within a foot or two the dimensions of every section of the excavations.

Twice Julie came in and she eyed Shelter haughtily, but with a sort of yearning that Shandy was quick to pick up.

"Jealous of that Middlesex woman, ain't she?" Shandy asked, but Shelter didn't see the point in answering.

Shell drank coffee, sitting alone at the table as sundown flooded the hills with color. D.D. had been fed in the other room and Shelter, Shandy and Julie had had a silent supper of beef and greens.

Now it was growing rapidly dark. Soon it would be time to go hunting. This time it would be different, however, this time they knew he would be coming. This time they would shoot to kill.

"Where's your badge?" Shandy asked.

"I lost it last night," Shell said. He explained about stuffing his shirt in the stovepipe. "I really wasn't worried about removing the badge when I did it."

"Hell of a thing," Shandy said, wagging his head as he walked away. "Hell of a thing for a lawman to do to his badge."

Sundown was a brilliant display of crimson and deep purple across the mountains. The few high clouds held the stain of color long after the skies had turned black and the stars had begun to sparkle across the distances of space.

Shelter Morgan slipped from the house an hour later, although he felt it was too early. He would have preferred to wait until long after midnight when the guards' eyes grew heavy, when they became bored with their task and sought only to keep warm as the night slowly rolled toward sunrise.

But Shandy was more impatient. He gave Shell a torn leather coat and returned his pistol. He gave him a last minute admonition to "shoot some of those buzzards" and stood watching as Morgan filtered off through the darkness, wondering what sort of mad pursuit this was, what kind of fool's game he was playing.

Hunting a town when he should be looking for Middlesex. Creeping across the night shadowed hills when he should be taking care of D.D.

What would it take to drive these men out of Massacre anyway, short of killing them all—a distasteful and unlikely plan?

Shell crept along the side of the hill, following the path he had taken the night before. There were few lights in Massacre on this evening. The wind was cold as it gusted up the long valleys.

He was suddenly upon a man. Shelter froze his motion, the night and dark coloration of his clothing concealing him briefly. He waited until he saw the shadowy head turn and then he ducked behind the roughly cut stump five feet away.

Peering up he saw the guard pace ten steps one way, then ten the other. The man breathed out volumes of steam and from time to time muttered a curse to himself. He was obviously cold and uncomfortable despite the big buffalo coat he wore. Shell hoped Middlesex was paying him enough to make this worth his while, but doubted it. These thugs who went into a fight-for-pay situation out of sheer laziness or the inability to do any decent, honest work were long between jobs, paid with a few quickly squandered dollars and expected to lay their lives on the line for the boss.

It was a wonder there were so many of them, would always be so many.

Shell waited until the man's back was turned and then he rose from the cover of the stump. He took four quick steps, lifted his Colt and brought the barrel down sharply behind the outlaw's ear.

The man caved in. He sagged to the earth without a whimper. Shell rolled him over, took his gunbelt and pistol, set his rifle aside, and then as a bonus, removed the big buffalo coat, slipping into it quickly.

He yanked the man's belt and shirt off, used the belt to bind his feet and the shirt to tie his hands behind his back, knotting a tight figure "8" which he had yet to see anyone wriggle out of. With one sleeve torn from the shirt he gagged the man, leaving him in a water cut hollow fifteen feet upslope. There he would be out of the sight of searching eyes for a good long while.

Shell tried the outlaw's hat on, found it much too large and sailed it away. Now he left the trail and climbed higher, knowing they were watching it—perhaps having found his bootprints during the day.

It was a good thing he had left the trail because another hundred yards along he spotted a second guard, perched on a rock, chin on his hand, gloomily surveying the dark canyons and the dimly lighted barracks.

It would have been easier to slip around this guard, but Shelter reasoned he might want to return this way and it was better to have all the opposition out of the way.

He eased down the slope, stopping cold as a stone was dislodged from underfoot and rolled down the hill. The guard heard nothing.

He saw nothing minutes later when Shell cracked him on the skull with the butt of the Winchester he had appropriated. Shell hastily tied this second man, lifting his gunbelt as well.

He was nearly finished tying him up when he saw a shadow against the starlight and he whirled, Colt coming up.

"No." The voice was low, somehow familiar.

Casco stepped from out of the darkness, looked once at Morgan, then bent over and picked up the outlaw. Tossing him effortlessly over his shoulder the big Indian turned and walked away.

Upslope Shelter could see a horse, and slung over the back of it was the first guard. Shelter supposed he had himself a deputy.

But he needed more than a deputy, he needed an army of men. That became starkly obvious when, a few minutes later, he crawled to the edge of a cold, damp outcropping and looked down into the town of Massacre where a dozen armed men patrolled the streets.

9.

The situation was simply impossible. Armed patrols moved through the streets of Massacre, and at the first shot from Morgan they would return his fire with a fury reminiscent of Bull Run. The hell with Shandy, the hell with Massacre! He was pulling out while he was in one piece.

That seethed inside him for a time, and he had half a notion to do it, but it wasn't easy to get over the final objection to pulling out—they had D.D.

He supposed there had to be a way to go about this, but he was damned if he knew what it was just then. Pulling back from the lip of the rocky ledge Shell found a shadowed hollow in which to sit and turn the problem over. It was Colonel Fainer himself who once said there were no military obstacles which the proper tactics properly executed could not overcome.

Well, Fainer had never seen an obstacle the size of this one, Shell decided. Inspiration was supposed to come at a time like this, but Shelter felt no warm glow of inspiration, only cold helplessness.

He watched the men below him, measuring their rounds; watching for a long hour he saw nothing that would help him in the least.

He rose again only to be moving, to keep the stiffness from settling into his bones. He had kept a wary eye out for Casco, but apparently his deputy had quit. A wise choice.

He crawled again to the edge of the outcropping. From there he could look almost straight down into Massacre. The barracks was fifty feet below him, and from time to time he was able to make out a man's face when he turned toward the light.

Inspiration. It slowly seeped into his mind. A mad, tenuous scheme began to take form and he hunkered down against the cold stone, turning it over in his mind to see how it shaped up.

It meant a long, rugged detour, but looking toward the hills, Shelter figured he could make it all right. Possibly there were not even any guards posted here, behind and above the town. It would take a long climb to get up here, and in the darkness a sentry wouldn't see far enough to make it worth while.

Deciding suddenly he crawled back to the hillside, and when he was out of the line of sight, he stood and climbed into the timber above the town.

It was an hour's slow work but he made it finally to the yawning mouth of the mine. No one stood guard there—why would they?

Shelter moved cautiously anyway, slipping undetected into the mine where he stood studying the town from that angle for a time before emerging, crossing to the sheds Shandy had described standing on a small ledge fifty feet farther along and down.

The moon was rising before Shelter returned to the ledge. A pale crescent moon peering cautiously over the jagged, black line of the mountains to the east. It cast a shadow before Shell as he circled back to his point of attack, carrying his burden.

He crawled to the edge of the outcropping again, cold sweat cooling his body. He noticed that there were just as many guards as before despite the late hour and he silently cursed.

He could smell the cold ashes of the burned out saloon, see the light in the barracks. He watched as a man lit another guard's cigarette and listened, not quite catching the words they spoke to each other before each turned and stomped off up the muddy, dark street, the moon throwing crooked shadows out from their feet.

Shelter went back to his parcel and removed thirteen sticks of dynamite. He fused them up, tied them together with strips torn from his shirt, and picked up the coil of rope.

Tucking the dynamite inside his shirt he knotted the hemp rope around a granite knob and eased over the side of the ledge, half expecting to be shot as he dangled there. But the moon, smiling kindly upon this effort perhaps, graciously slipped behind a ragged cloud and the night grew dimmer.

Shell eased down the rope, his hands cramping as he lowered himself. He had time to wonder again what kind of fool he was before he had accomplished the fifty foot descent and he found himself crouched against the dark earth between the overhanging ledge and the barracks.

A guard circled the barracks and Shelter went to his belly, flattening himself against the cold, damp earth. If the man saw that rope dangling from the ledge . . . but there was nothing he could do about that but hope.

The hour was late and the night cold. The guard was more intent on keeping warm as he passed by Shelter, the slow plodding of his feet audible.

When the guard had gone around the corner of the barracks Shelter moved, quickly, surely setting his charge. He placed it at the base of the outcropping, looking over his shoulder constantly to make sure he was not caught.

And then he was through. Perspiration beaded his forehead. His head pulsed with blood. The night felt suddenly warm and he shed the encumbering buffalo coat. He was going to have to climb and climb fast.

Bending low Shelter struck his match which seemed unnaturally bright in the night. The fuse caught immediately with a hiss and a spurt of white sparks.

Shelter caught his rope and began climbing furiously. Every moment counted. If the guard came around the building again, the fuse would be bound to draw his eyes. The man on the rope would be a dead pigeon.

If the fuse was too quick, Shelter was liable to be blown off of that rock and buried under the rubble—that spurred him on to greater exertions. His shoulders were fiery, his chest gasping for oxygen. He climbed, expecting at any moment the jarring impact of a rifle bullet or the shattering, deadly explosion of dynamite, enough to blast him all the way to

Sutler's Flats. Or to Hades.

He was nearly to the top, had only to stretch out his hand and roll up and over the ledge when he heard a shout.

"Hey someone's up on the ledge!"

A shot rang out, splintering the rock under Shell's clawing hand. Fragments of rock exploded into his flesh and with anger he felt the rush of hot blood.

Another shot sang off the face of the outcropping and another, but then he was up and over, running in a crouch across the ledge. He snatched up the rifle he had left there and ran on, trying to outrace disaster. He hit the timber at a dead run and wove his way upward, his ears tuned expectantly . . . but no sound followed him.

Had they found the dynamite! It was too slow, too slow. It should have gone by now.

And then it did. With a force which nearly knocked Shelter off his feet so that he had to cling to the massive lodgepole pine beside him.

The earth trembled and exploded with a deafening sound which rattled his ear drums. And then great jutting tongues of crimson and yellow-white fire flared up against the night.

And slowly, as Shelter could see from his vantage point, the ledge itself buckled and sloughed off, sliding down into Massacre with a tremendous, rolling rumble. Through the smoke and the dust, the lingering tendrils of flame Shell watched as the ledge collapsed; thousands of tons of stone hung momentarily in space and then thundered down.

The barracks and anyone standing near it was swept away in the avalanche. Stone flooded Massacre's main street, huge jagged boulders bounded high into the air and struck other buildings, tearing them to kindling.

And then, like that, it was over. There was only the dust, the sharp scent of dynamite smoke in the air. It became utterly still. The silence was broken only by an occasional stone rushing to join the avalanche, pinging off the already fallen stone.

And then, in the silence, it was possible to hear the moaning of a wounded man far below. It was not a pleasant sound and Shell shuttled off through the trees, entering the darkness again, moving like a dark ghost.

James Middlesex was livid. The skin was drawn back tautly over his Indian cheekbones. His dark eyes burned with subdued fire. He was a man ready to explode. At dawn he arrived in Massacre, his fully developed plan for taking over the Shandy mine ready to be executed.

Then, topping the ridge he had halted his horse with amazement. He sat staring at the town in white-lipped rage. The saloon was no longer there. It had been burned to the ground.

He was about to curse the gunmen he had hired for their stupid carelessness when he noticed that the barracks no longer existed either. A mountain of stone lay on the site.

His few remaining men he found huddled together around a small campfire beside a small standing building which had once been Massacre's barber shop.

Red Coyle glanced up from the fire, his broad face

reflecting a knowledge of the dressing-down to come. Middlesex wasn't just angry, he was white with fury.

"This might be worse than everything else," Coyle whispered to the man who stood beside him. Coyle rose, dusting off his hands. "Morning, boss," he managed before Middlesex broke into a frothing, cursing nearly apoplectic tirade.

With Coyle and the mustached, sharp featured Tex Chambers Middlesex surveyed the town as the sun lifted above the eastern mountains, gilding the tips of the pines. It was a beautiful, clear morning. Middlesex noticed none of the beauty.

"Two nights ago we found the barracks on fire," Red explained as they picked their way up the rubble clotted street. "At least we thought it was on fire. Turns out someone had climbed up and stuffed a shirt in the stovepipe."

Middlesex nodded impatiently. They could see the hand of a man protruding from under tons of gray rock. His rifle lay nearby.

"So," Red went on with a nervous glance at Tex Chambers who looked back sympathetically, "we come out to put out the barracks and the saloon was torched. Went up in half an hour, I'd say."

"Didn't you see anybody?" Middlesex demanded.

"I did," Red answered. "Don't know who it was. Tall man, me and him scuffled in the alley in back of the saloon. He got away."

"Tell him about last night," Tex prodded. Middlesex's cold glare silenced Tex. They had stopped in front of the mound of stone which was piled up to a height of thirty feet or more.

"There's not a lot to tell, Mister Middlesex. Someone set a charge, and you can see the result. We lost four men in the barracks, two in the street."

"And Bill and Foster," Tex put in.

"What happened to them?" Middlesex asked. Could it get any worse?

"I don't rightly know," Red said, removing his hat to wipe back his thinning red hair. "They were posted up on the hill as sentries. They never came back, though Foster's horse wandered in just before daybreak."

"And Ed Lucy and them," Tex said.

"Yeah," Red spat into the dust as they turned back upstreet. "Ed and three of those California boys said they'd had enough. No pay, their gear buried under that rock. They took off on us."

"If I ever see those bastards again . . ." Middlesex began. Then his jaw clamped shut. "Who was it, Red? Who hit us? It couldn't have been Shandy. That damned Indian of his?"

"It wasn't the Indian. It was dark in the alley, but not that dark. No, it was someone I never seen before. Let me show you something, boss."

Middlesex watched with barely concealed irritability as Red fished in his coat pocket and withdrew a metallic object. Middlesex's eyes narrowed. It was a star.

"The law? How . . . from where?" He took the star and turned it over. "U.S. marshal?" he asked Red who was familiar with all sorts of badges from first-hand experience.

"Naw, it's some kind of townie's badge," Red answered. "Though since we ain't got a town or a

122

town marshal, I don't figure it. There's no marshal in Sutler's Flats?"

"No." Middlesex was preoccupied. He handed the badge back. "Where'd you find it, Red?"

"On the shirt that was stuffed into the stovepipe. And there was one other thing. Guess it don't mean much, it don't seem to anyway."

"What is it?"

Red handed him the folded, soot stained piece of paper. It was blackened, weathered and streaked but it was readable and Middlesex looked at it with trembling hands. Red had thought Middlesex was already as mad as a man could get, but now, looking at that scrap of paper his face bleached white, his upper lip curled back in an involuntary sneer, his eyes bulged behind nearly closed eyelids.

Middlesex seemed to have forgotten that Red and Tex Chambers were with him. He stood in the middle of the street staring at the note which he held in both hands.

"Shell," the note read. "Watch yourself. The . . ."

Finally Middlesex came to himself. Those hooded eyes lifted to those of Red. "Describe the man in the alley again," he said coldly. His hands parted, still clenching the note. The old paper tore in half and Middlesex stood there rigidly, hands at his sides, staring at a point beyond Red Coyle. "Describe me that man, Red."

"Well, tall, like I said, maybe six-three. Lanky, dark hair. Straight nose. That was about all, except he's a fighting man. He showed me somethin' in the alley." Middlesex seemed not to be listening. "Does it mean something to you, Mister Middlesex?"

"Where is he?' Middlesex asked, his voice a hiss between clenched teeth. "Where is Shelter Morgan?"

"Who?"

"The tall man. His name is Morgan."

"Couldn't say, boss," Red said. He and Tex Chambers exchanged glances. Middlesex looked like a man not quite in control of himself. His jaw muscles were rigid and there was a slight tic below his left eye. "That first night Foster reckoned he went back to the Shandy house. That figures, I guess. What is he, some hired gun? Some friend of Shandy's?"

"He's a dead man," James Middlesex said. "That's what he is—a dead man. We're going up there, Red."

"To Shandy's?"

"To Shandy's. We're going to finish this all off right now. Finish Shandy, finish Morgan. All of it. Get your men together, Red."

"You know," Tex put in timidly, "that Shandy girl can shoot like nothin' I ever saw, and there ain't no way to approach that house without . . ."

"Now!" Middlesex hadn't heard Tex at all. He was looking into the distances. Toward Georgia. It was him or Morgan now. The man would never let him live. The mine suddenly became secondary. Shelter Morgan filled his thoughts. Only one thing mattered—Morgan must die.

10.

"Something's up," Shelter said. He had been looking out the door and now he turned back toward Jack Shandy who was enjoying a leisurely breakfast. "They're having some sort of a conference in the middle of town. They've got their horses."

"Think they're coming up, do you?" Shandy asked as if unconcerned by any of this. He dabbed at his goat whiskers with his napkin.

"It's possible," Shelter answered. "Where else would they be going. I doubt they're pulling out."

"I doubt it too. You'll have to clean 'em all out before they do that."

"Shandy," Shelter said, his voice now taut with anger. "Have I told you that you're crazy. That you've got a lot of nerve blackmailing me, holding a decent woman hostage. That I couldn't care a hoot in a holler if they win or you do?"

Astonishingly Shandy chuckled. "No, you ain't said that, Morgan. But you didn't have to. I know how you feel—any man would feel that way. But it don't hurt my feelings. I'm trying to do what's right. Trying to protect my own interests." Shandy rose. He threw his napkin down on the table and continued, in a thoughtful voice which Shelter hadn't heard before.

"There was thirty armed men down there, Morgan. Against me and Casco and the girl. Now what in hell do you think the eventual outcome was going to be? They'd win. I'm not that crazy. They'd win and take it all away.

"But you think of this—that mine is all I have. I've labored fifteen years at it. And Julie, why she's had nothing all the time she was growing up. Hard tack and hard weather, lonely times and shabby clothes. Now I've hit paydirt and in a little while I'll be able to do for the girl. I'm an old man, Morgan, all I've got is my girl, and all I've got to leave her is the gold in that mine. You know what life is like out here for a girl with nothing.

"Yes, I kidnapped the Middlesex woman, yes I'm forcing you to risk your life, but do you know what—it don't bother me a bit when I look at the alternative."

He winked then and turned away, calling to the Indian. "Casco. Morgan thinks they're coming up after us now, and I agree. Take the woman and hide her in the hills."

The Indian nodded and without hesitation moved into the small back room, returning with D.D. She looked with pleading eyes to Shelter and just for a moment there he wanted to try it. He was armed. Shandy was not. Casco had a knife, but it was sheathed. D.D.'s imploring glance nudged him toward the attempt.

Draw, back off Shandy, get D.D. the hell out of there and make for Sutler's Flats. The sound of the rifle cocking was loud behind him.

"Go on now, Casco," Julie said. "Get that tramp out of here. Mister Morgan, you hold steady."

That Sharps would blow a hole in a man big enough for a buffalo to romp through. Shell held steady. The Indian strode past, dragging a defeated D.D. Short. Shandy risked a small satisfied smile.

"Now us, Julie. Mister Morgan will stay and hold off these outlaws."

Julie's face altered and assumed grim determination. "I'll not leave him, Pa."

"Julie!" Shandy spread his hands in a pleading gesture.

"Get now. You never could shoot, Pa."

"Not without you, girl."

"Then you'll have a long wait. He's my man, Pa. I'll not leave him."

Shelter smiled despite himself. Shandy looked baffled. He glanced from Shelter to Julie and back.

"Tell her, Morgan!" the old man demanded.

"You'd better go on along, Julie. I'd only have to worry about you," Shelter said.

"And me? If I go and leave you alone, I'll be worried sick about you. I can shoot! Why can't I stay?"

"It's better if I'm alone," Shell answered, looking across Julie's shoulder at Shandy who still wore a perplexed look. "I can fight and run, strike and withdraw. I'd have a better chance of surviving," he said and that was a convincing argument.

"If . . . if that's true," she said hesitantly.

"It is, Julie. Honestly it is."

"All right." She ran a hand across her dark, tumbling hair. "All right then. I'll go, but I don't like it. I'll go, but I'll be back for you, Shelter Morgan."

Then, to Shandy's astonishment she threw her arms around Morgan's shoulders and kissed him full on the mouth, a long, lingering kiss which Shell himself had to break off.

"Get," he said with a smile. He nodded at Shandy and the old man, still befuddled, took Julie by the arm and led her from the cabin.

That left Shelter alone. Alone against a small army, an unwilling mercenary in Shandy's battle. There was only one satisfaction in all of this—Morgan knew that those were Middlesex's men down there and realized that this was hurting Middlesex. To ruin his scheme, to crush his army would not repay the man, but it would hurt him badly. He had planned this carefully and for a long while, apparently.

Marry into the Short family, recruit an army, squeeze out Shandy. But it was the small points, the care taken which pointed to an extraordinary cunning—how did Middlesex know about this set-up in the first place? He would have to have known there was virtually no law up here, known Short had an unmarried daughter, known that he still held half the claim.

All of that could have been learned through public records, and probably was, but it took a bit of dark imagination, of animal intelligence to put it together, to coldly stalk the girl and the gold.

It would not be wise to underestimate Mister James Middlesex, not wise at all.

Shelter had moved out onto the porch and now he sat crouched, his back against the house wall, watching the activity in the canyon below.

They were a bit too far off to be made out clearly, but there was something about the man in the suit, the man who rode at the head of the band of men slowly filing out of Massacre, threading their way up the trail to the Shandy house. And suddenly Shell *knew*.

He couldn't see the man clearly, but something about him, the way he sat a horse perhaps, jogged a deep memory and he knew.

Who else would be wearing a town suit, riding at the head of these outlaws, anyway? It was him. James Middlesex and throwing out his first plan to let them draw close, Morgan lifted his Winchester, placed the barrel across the porch railing, settled the black iron bead sight on the gray coat of Middlesex, four inches to the right of center, took in a slow breath, held it and squeezed.

The rifleshot racketed down the long canyon. Shelter saw Middlesex swat at his shoulder, saw his white horse rear up in wild-eyed panic, and he knew two things simultaneously—he had hit Middlesex, but he had not hit him well. Cursing the unfamiliar rifle which shot high and right, Shelter jacked another .44-40 into the chamber and again he fired, trying for the big, red-haired man on Middlesex's left.

He missed cleanly this time, and now the outlaws were firing back with everything they had. Bullets slammed into eaves and the wall behind Shelter, some whined off into the woods beyond. The rocker sitting on the porch was turned around by bullets and shattered to splinters.

Shell took off at a run as the outlaws drove up the trail from Massacre, leaning low across their horses' necks, firing a hail of red hot lead.

Bullets tore up the planking at Shelter's feet, and his bootheel was nearly jerked from under him as a bullet ticked off it. He left the porch in a headlong dive, hurling himself toward the timber beyond the Shandy house.

He hit the ground, jarring the breath from his lungs, rolled to his feet and staggered on, zig-zagging through the pines. He stopped, panting, hearing the driving thud of horses' hooves on the trail, a single exultant yell, a curse.

They couldn't ride that fast in the timber, he knew, and he supposed they would figure him to be running for the hills. Knowing that, he doubled back, sifting through the trees on a course parallel to but fifty feet west of the trail he had broken entering the woods.

The first of the pursuing horsemen was already into the trees. Shell dropped behind a screen of scrub oak, holding himself ready as the man, a burly, black bearded outlaw, spurred his pony into the timber.

His eyes flickered toward the cover where Shell lay, but he did not see him. He was looking for a running man, expecting one and his senses betrayed him.

Shell let him pass. The outlaw slowed his horse as

they entered the forest and Shell made his move. He darted across the space between them like a shadow flitting through the woods, and he leaped up, hitting the man high.

They sprawled to the ground, and Shell brought his fist down once, twice. Black beard didn't move. Shell heard pounding hoofs behind him and turned just as the man on the pale horse fired with his Winchester.

From the saddle of a shying horse it was a tough shot and he missed, the bullet slapping off the trunk of a pine and singing off through the trees.

Shell didn't miss. From one knee he palmed his Colt and fired twice, both shots dead center above the left breast pocket of the man's shirt. He slumped from the saddle, and as his panicked horse took off at a dead run, he hit the ground and was dragged off through the trees, one foot caught in the stirrup. His dead eyes were wide open, seemingly looking with amazement at Shell as his mount thundered past.

Shell turned, ducked into the brush again and waited, letting three men pass by. It was Middlesex he wanted, only Middlesex.

A shout suddenly went up.

"Over here!" The voice was triumphant and Shell turned to see the red-haired man, the one he had tussled with in the alley nearly on top of him, his big bay horse foam-flecked, wide eyed as he was steered toward Morgan.

Shell pressed himself against the tree and felt the grazing impact of the horse's shoulder. He tumbled to the earth, feeling with panic his pistol fly free of his hand. Now, as Red turned for another assault,

Shell could see other outlaws driving through the trees to join him.

Red was nearly on top of him again and Shell rolled to one side, trying for his Colt, not finding it. Suddenly there was the boom of a large bore rifle and Red, looking at Morgan with pained surprise, toppled from the saddle, a hole through the center of his chest.

Who?—Looking upslope Shelter saw Julie, the muzzle of her Sharps curling smoke, waving frantically to him. He snatched up his pistol and took off at a dead run, throwing two wild shots across his shoulder to slow the pursuit.

"What are you doing here!" Shell gasped as he reached Julie.

"And aren't you glad I am," she snapped back. "Come on, Morgan."

"Not that way." Julie had started toward the house again, and Shell knew they would never make it. "Toward the mine."

She started to argue, clamped her jaw shut, raised her rifle and took a man from the saddle at a hundred yards, reloaded and tossed her head proudly. "You're the boss," she said with a taunting mockery in her words.

They ran upslope for another five hundred yards, dipped into a brush clotted hollow where the brambles tore at their exposed flesh, then they were onto a cleared slope. Ahead lay Massacre, and up the shale littered slope, the entrance to Shandy Mine.

They scrambled up over the loose shale and rubble from the mine. Julie fell once, sliding back thirty feet, her rifle clattering free, and Shell had to crawl back to help her up, firing twice at the pursuit which had bogged down in the dense thicket along the hollow.

Still, remarkably, he hit a man. His scream echoed across the slope. Julie, muttering astonishingly unladylike expletives was yanked to her feet and with Shell she clambered toward the entrance to the mine.

They hit the mine at a dead run, the rifle shots ringing off the stone around them, tearing at the timbers.

"Get down," Shell ordered and Julie hit the deck, Shelter beside her. Crawling back to the mine entrance which was still being peppered with lead, he waited until the first horsemen broke free of the brush and then he emptied his pistol in that direction, seeing a nearly black horse crumple up, its knees buckling as it pitched its rider free and slowly rolled over, skidding downslope on the slide of shale, its hooves pawing at the air as its desperate whinnying filled the air.

Julie, in a prone position picked off a man who was creeping upslope from the Massacre side. He clutched at his forehead, threw his arms wide and then disappeared over a steep cut.

"We could hold them here forever, if . . ." Julie said.

"If?" Shell looked at her and with a pained smile she held out her palm, revealing one blunt nosed .50 caliber cartridge.

"That's all I've got."

"Christ," Shell muttered.

"Exactly," Julie said.

"What the hell are you doing here anyway," he

133

asked angrily. "I thought you were with your father."

"You needed me," she said with a mixture of satisfaction and anger. "You're my man."

Shelter didn't take the time to respond. The outlaws were charging upslope now, riding Indian style. He furiously shovelled fresh loads into his Colt, emptied it, scoring one hit and reloaded again. The loops in his gunbelt were getting mighty empty. At this range with a handgun he would be lucky to score one hit in ten.

But his eyes were alert for James Middlesex. He wanted the man. Discounting the fact that there was bad blood between them, Shelter knew that to tag Middlesex might take the fire out of his men. After all, they were fighting for wages and when the paymaster went down there wasn't a lot of sense left in fighting.

But he couldn't spot Middlesex. He wondered hopefully if the bullet he had put into the badman had done more damage than it appeared.

Julie screamed. Somehow an outlaw had gotten on the bank above the mine entrance and he had dropped down in front of it, his eyes blazing. She touched off instantly, that buffalo gun blowing a hole the size of Shell's fist through his chest. The man was thrown back as if jerked by invisible wires, his blood spattering them and Julie, uncharacteristically broke into tears.

Maybe she had never killed a man at close range before. There's a hell of a difference.

Shelter had seen men in war, some of his best sharpshooters, suddenly balk when an enemy soldier, a real living man at close range suddenly appeared before them. Picking off targets in the distance had seemed a sort of a game to them. To look into a living man's eyes, to see details of expression, of features—it had a way of bringing it all home, of underlining that what you were doing was killing, that this man before you was a real human being with every emotion you possessed, with family and friends, desires, ambitions, fears. Some men, too sensitive to do it, had forfeited their own lives instead of instinctively squeezing off the saving shot.

"Come on." Shell wrapped an arm around Julie. There was blood on her white blouse front, a bright speck of it on her throat.

"Where?" she seemed very young suddenly, very frightened.

"Back." He nodded his head toward the interior of the mine.

"But there's no way out!"

"We can't stay here." Even as Shelter spoke a hail of bullets reached the entrance of the mine shaft, the bullets ricocheting madly off the stone, tearing themselves to jagged, white hot missiles.

"Come on!" he shouted above the din and she could not answer. Crawling back a ways, Shell got to his feet. It was darker, cooler as they withdrew.

Julie stumbled along beside him, her feet dragging, her shoulders trembling. Shell crouched, pausing. He held Julie against the wall behind him as his eyes fixed on the sunbright entrance to the mine.

Two men appeared and he levelled four shots at them. That would give them something to think about. It would be a time before anyone tried the entrance again.

"Let's go. That'll only hold them for a time."

Shell liked none of this. He didn't give himself a chance to think about it, but it nagged him. Trapped inside a hole in the earth with a young woman. It was a bad, very bad tactical situation. Defensively they were all right. A man would have to be insane to step in there after them.

On the other hand—there was no way out. They were short on ammunition, and more importantly had no water and food.

A rifle shot, seeming both distant and very close sounded loud in the cavern, echoing down the tunnel. Hot lead pinged off the walls, taking random angles as it searched for them.

There was a small stope not fifty feet on, Shell recalled from Shandy's diagrams. They would be safe there temporarily—if they could find it.

Darkness assumed a dominant role now as they went deeper into the heart of the mine. Shelter felt Julie trip and start to go down and he had to yank her to her feet. An unseen rock had tripped her. How many such obstacles were there? How many pits and dead ends?

Shelter tried to recall all he had learned from Shandy, but it was little enough—the man had been recalcitrant, and at times, it seemed to Shell, he had told out and out lies, trying to protect his gold. Now, because of that, he was liable to lose a daughter.

Bullets swarmed down the corridors, striking red sparks where they ricocheted off stone. Their whining was the song of angry, deadly hornets. Shell and Julie flattened out against the cold floor of the dark mine, each knowing that it was only a matter of time before they were hit.

During a brief lull in the firing they got to their feet and scrambled on. Rounding an elbow bend in the shaft they found the stope.

A hollow with its ledge six feet above the floor of the shaft, it offered some safety and they scrambled up into it, Shelter grabbing Julie by the wrist to lift her up and into the stope.

Again the fearsome fusilade began. Bullets flying blindly through the darkness struck sparks, scattered flying splinters of stone, bit angrily at the timbers.

Shell and Julie pressed back against the farthest wall of the stope, and he held her head to his chest, the sweat streaming from his forehead, dust clinging to his face as the bullets flew.

Suddenly it was still. Still, utterly dark and quite deadly.

"What's happened?" Julie asked. He could not even see her face in the darkness.

"I don't know."

But he had an idea. An idea he didn't like a bit. "Julie, is there some way out of here besides the way we came?"

"No," she answered, but there was a hesitation in her voice which puzzled him.

"In that case, we're in a real jam," he said.

"Why? What do you mean." Her words were taut with panic.

He didn't answer her. He didn't have time to before the deafening boom shook the stone walls of the cavern and the dust rolled through the shaft, followed by a hot gust of wind.

The rolling trembling continued for long minutes. The dust clotted their nostrils and mouths. Stone fell from up above, one head-sized rock narrowly missing Shell.

"What. . . ?" Julie asked, but she knew. She already knew what had happened and there was no need for Shelter to explain that Middlesex had dynamited the entrance to the Shandy mine, sealing them up in a tomb from which there was no escape.

11.

The dust slowly settled. Already the air in the mine seemed close and stale. Julie huddled against Shelter Morgan, unmoving, unspeaking. Shell's head still rang with the echoes of the explosion.

Well, this was it then, he thought. He had bought it finally. How many times, in how many places had he flirted with it? Toyed with death, expecting it to end suddenly with a burst of gunfire, with the sudden searing impact of a bullet, with a sudden tumble into a dark, bottomless tunnel.

But this . . . this was enough to strike terror into anyone's heart. To sit there and slowly suffocate, to slowly die. In darkness and in silence. Hours would pass, perhaps days and there was nothing a man could do but sit and ponder the error of his ways, and watch Death slowly shuffling toward him, his scythe poised to cut the life from under him.

He sat there in stony lethargy, eyes closed, feeling the quick pulse of Julie's heart as he held her tightly, breathing in the dusty air, feeling the cold embrace of dying.

How long they waited, soundlessly for it, he could not later say. Maybe the explosion had concussed him, maybe the sheer force and viciousness of it had undermined hope.

He sat brooding, his thoughts dark, his heart a cold stone, regretful only because of the young woman beside him. He had made his run; she had not. She had seen nothing of life but a shabby, leaky mountain cabin, a bleak, stony wilderness, cold winters and poor food.

She had probably never had a new dress, never been able to go to those country dances and flirt with the boys. All of that lay ahead of her . . . or it had.

Shelter came suddenly alert, anger flooding him. An anger against the man whose greed caused all of this. He stood outside right now, no doubt, perhaps lighting a cigar, telling his men that they needed only to wait a day or two and reopen the mine.

"Julie!" He shook her shoulder and she muttered sleepily. The air was bad in the mine already, very bad. To fall asleep might be to sleep forever. He shook her harder.

"Julie!"

"Wasit?"

"Wake up, we've got to keep moving."

"Werzamovto?"

"Julie!" He held her at arm's length and slapped her cheek. The sound of the blow landing rang loudly in the close confines of the stope. "We've got to get moving. Do something." He stood and lifted her. "Come on!"

She was awake enough to stay on her feet, but that

was about it. Shelter had no firm idea of what he might do, but he knew something must be done if possible. The alternative was to sit in the stope and die by suffocation.

He had a vague hope of tunneling back out. They wouldn't expect that and maybe they wouldn't be watching. Maybe it would be dark—that would help. *Maybe* they would emerge, take a bullet in the heart and die.

Even that seemed preferable to a lingering death, to a slow strangling of the lungs.

As they moved slowly back toward the entrance to the mine, Shell keeping his hand on the wall of the shaft to guide him, it became suddenly, starkly obvious that the plan was utter foolishness.

They came abruptly to a wall of stone. It had caved in deeply. There was a hundred feet of stone between them and the shaft entrance. Shell felt along the wall of rock, desperately searching for some opening. There was none and he turned away, feeling bitter frustration.

"Julie?" He had lost her and had to hunt for her with his hands, using her labored breathing for a guide. She did not answer. "Are there any air shafts back farther? Any ventilators?" He could recall none in Shandy's diagrams.

"What?"

"Back farther are there any ventilating shafts?"

"I don't know. Yes . . . no." He could feel her shrug. "Maybe."

"Well, that covers all the possibilities, doesn't it?" he asked, angry not with her but with the situation. He had out-foxed himself good this time. He should have known better than to get himself trapped like this.

"Let's go," he said with a sigh.

"Where . . ." her voice was shrill with strain.

"Anywhere. Back that way. Anywhere but here." They moved deeper into the black tunnel of the mineshaft. They crept forward a step at a time like two blind people. Twice Shelter had to yank up on Julie's arm to keep her from falling over unseen obstacles.

Moments later Shelter himself went down hard, pulling Julie with him. His face smashed against the stone floor and he felt his chin split open.

Rising they struggled on. The air was rancid now, breathing a chore. Shelter tried to recall that diagram of Shandy's, tried to measure distances with his stride. Somewhere up ahead there was a bend in the shaft . . . he laughed out loud. Did it matter which fork they took! Either led to death.

It was half an hour's walk to the fork in the shaft, and for no reason at all Shelter took the right extension. He had taken six steps into it when the floor was swept away from under foot and he was falling, falling.

Split seconds later he was met by icy, devouring liquid.

He had fallen into a pit filled with slimy water. He went under before he could take a breath and ended up swallowing a pint of the rancid liquid.

He came up coughing and choking, frozen to the bone. He had *known* it was there. He had known it, or should have. He recalled it from Shandy's diagram. He had known it, but his oxygen starved brain had neglected to inform his feet.

Walked right into it . . . and now how in hell was he going to get up? It was twenty feet to the rim, or so he recalled. In the darkness it might have been half a mile.

He treaded water for a minute, his arms moving in sweeping circles. When he could speak he shouted up the shaft. "Julie!"

"Where are you?" she called nonsensically. Her thinking had been fuzzy with the bad air for a long while now. It was getting no better.

"Can you throw something down?"

A cantaloupe-sized rock splashed into the water nearly crushing Shell's skull.

"Stop!" he cried out in panic and exasperation. "I need a line. A rope. Anything to help me out."

Did she understand? There was utter silence from above and only cold, black water below. He could see absolutely nothing. If there was any way at all to climb out of the pit it was useless to Shelter. He could only wait, the cold water draining his strength, hoping that the message had gotten through to Julie's ravaged consciousness, hoping that somehow she could find something to help him.

But the minutes passed and no help was forthcoming. From time to time he heard a faint, indefinable sound, but there was nothing else.

Shell could feel the strength going from his arms and legs. To conserve himself he floated on his back for a time, head thrown far back. Bits of slime and muck floated into his mouth and once a dead, bloated rat nudged his cheek.

"Hey. Julie! Are you there?"

There was no answer as there had been none to a hundred previous calls. Shelter closed his eyes in frustration. He floated through blackness, had been floating through it for a hundred centuries. All of the world, all of the universe was only blackness, stinking, damp blackness . . .

Something splashed into the water not far from his feet and he came upright, grasping for it.

He found it. A length of knotted canvas, it seemed to be. "Julie? Is it secured?"

No answer again. If he tugged before she had the line secured he would simply pull it into the tank and throwing it out again while treading water was not so simple.

Finally, worrying about the girl now, he tested the length of material. He found it fast. It was knotted at intervals and as he climbed it held although from time to time there was an ominous tearing sound.

It seemed a lifetime's effort before slimy, shoulder weary, cold and wet he managed to drag himself up and over the lip of the tank.

He rolled free and lay there panting. A small voice reached for him out of the darkness.

"Shelter?"

"It's me. It's me or what's left of me," he said. And then she was on the ground beside him, clinging to him and Shell's hands discovered that she was naked. The cloth had been her jeans and shirt, the small sounds the sound of her tearing the cloth.

"I'm so stupid," she murmured, "I couldn't think of any other way."

"Stupid! If it hadn't been for that idea I'd have drowned in that tank, Julie. I don't think I've ever heard anything more clever. I'll admire your superior intelligence forever."

She laughed and held him more tightly. She was shivering and Shelter wondered which of them was the colder just then.

"I started off to look for a rope," Julie said, "down the other shaft where Pa had a winch. I couldn't find one, but the air is better, much better."

"Good. Let's see what we've got then," Shelter said, trying to keep his voice light and confident. The truth was he was strangling on the musty air here and he had barely the strength to make it to his feet. He took Julie's hand and stumbled along beside her, dripping water on the floor of the shaft, hoping against hope that the girl was right, that there was better air along the left hand shaft.

And she was right.

Rounding the last elbow in the shaft Shell felt a rush of cool, oxygen-sweet air and he sucked it greedily into his lungs. His head swam with it, his blood raced—there was nothing on earth so delightful. Let them have their juicy steaks, their liquor, their women! That air topped everything.

He leaned against the wall of the cavern, content just to breathe. Slowly he inhaled and exhaled, forgetting for the moment that he was cold, wet and trapped in a tunnel.

He was alive now, and he would stay alive for a time.

Julie had her head thrown back and Shell watched her . . . watched her! It was a time before that soaked in. He could see her!

That meant that not only air but light was leaking into the cave. If it could filter in, could they get out?

"Julie?" he gasped. "Where is it?"

"What—where's what?" She turned toward him and in the murky darkness he could see her expression slowly alter. "It's lighter in here."

"Yes, it is." Shelter walked slowly along the shaft, peering upward. "What is it? Some kind of ventilating shaft, what!"

"It's . . ." she fell silent. Shelter took her by her arms and gripped her tightly.

"It's what! This is no time for secrets."

"All right! There's another entrance to this mine. Pa told me never to whisper a word of it to anyone."

"Where? Where is it?" Shelter had resumed his search of the cavern roof. He could see the light coming in, but peering upward he could not find the source of it.

"That's it," Julie said. She sagged to the earth and simply sat there, cross-legged, naked, exhausted. "There's a hatch up there, made of planks. Over that brush is piled."

Shelter was angry, but his joy overcame that. She could have told him before and saved an icy soaking, a period of suffocation and near-panic. Yet he had to admire her in a way. Her father had told her never to mention it, and she had remained loyal even under these conditions.

Shell looked up. With his outstretched hand he could nearly reach the narrow, crooked opening. He could feel the draft on his palm, see pale yellow light from some source above.

"How much of a climb is it?" he asked.

146

"I don't know." Julie waved a weary hand.

"We'll have to wait until dark," Shell decided. "I'd hate to pop my head up and be looking up the muzzle of someone's gun. Does Middlesex know about this?"

"Ken Short didn't even know," Julie said. "Pa dug this shaft by himself and he met this natural shaft—water must have carved it out. He kept it secret, knowing he might need it one day if there was a cave-in. It was also kind of an insurance against an Indian attack."

"He must have had a ladder, someway of getting up there."

"I don't know."

"Handholds—did he chip handholds in the stone."

Again. "I don't know."

Shelter tried to look up the shaft which was no more than twenty-four inches long by thirty wide. He simply couldn't see. Shandy, of course, would have had a lantern with him. He did not.

"Shouldn't there be some lanterns down here?" Shell asked. Julie didn't answer. He moved off down the shaft a way, finding nothing. Probably there were lanterns in the other passage, but in the darkness he would never find them.

"How would you light it?" Julie asked and Shelter gave up the idea.

One way or another, however, he was going up once it got dark. If he fell in the attempt and broke his neck, it was too damned bad. It beat the alternative.

He sat beside Julie, stripping off his slimy shirt.

She sat tailor-fashion, her head hung, her arms inert. Then suddenly her face turned toward his.

"This is a terrible place. I feel like I'm going to die here . . . everything is closing in."

"We'll get out." He put his arm around her.

Suddenly, astonishingly she flung herself against him. "Hold me, Shelter Morgan. Hold me. It's so dark and empty in here. It's like the end of the world and I don't like it. Make the darkness go away."

She clung to him, her hand resting on his chest. Shelter kissed her then deeply, passionately and he felt her shudder. Slowly they lay back against the cold stone of the shaft, clinging together.

Julie sat up and with a deal of effort pulled Shelter's sodden boots off. He unbuckled his belt and she slipped his pants off over his ankles.

She lay down again and their bodies, cool and clammy, met. They had become savage. Lying together in a dark cave, naked and cold with only their own body heat to keep the chill from them.

They were as primitive as the first men who ever walked the earth. Men without fire, who hid in a deep winter cave while great savage beasts waited outside to devour them. Still a man had had a woman to cling to, to divert his thoughts from the world's harshness. And it must have been good for those long-ago cave dwellers, because it was damned good for Shell and Julie.

As their bodies heated, as Shell found her damp, inner warmth with his fingers, as she clung to his masculinity, her hands working fervently on his shaft, he forgot completely about Middlesex, about the cold and the battle ahead. Let the beasts outside

148

stalk and growl, he had her breasts next to his lips, had the warmth of her thighs pressed to his, had her eager mouth attacking his throat, face and chest, had her hands drawing him to her, her legs slowly spreading, the sudden, sweet warmth of her closing around him.

She lay on her back and Shell's hands slipped beneath her, clinging to the soft strength of her buttocks as she thrust high, and he rode her with a fierce concentration, his thinking only a matter of physical sensuality, his worries being driven away by the incredible, lithe machine which was the demanding, hip-swaying, rolling, grasping vitality of Julie Shandy.

She gripped him tightly and tugged at him, worked him in wide sweeping circles, suddenly clapping against him with incredible strength and timing.

She murmured something deep in her throat and her swaying abruptly ceased although Shell continued to rock against her, to bury himself in her, to grind against her. Her mouth was open and she was panting hard, and it was not from lack of oxygen now. She felt herself swell, flood and burst as Shelter tried to split her open. Julie threw her legs around him, her heels resting on the hard muscles of his buttocks, and she pressed him to her, pressed her breasts to his lips, feeling the tingling, grow, the sudden rush of hot fluid, the incredible tailspin into sensuality beyond sensation.

She was enveloped by hot rushing winds, turned around and spun by washes of color, and she felt as if she were going to be turned inside out as he drove against her, as he penetrated again and again, his

149

body rigid, his excitement evident.

Her hands dropped between her legs and with two fingers she touched his erection as it slammed into her. Her head had begun a wild spinning and she felt that she was suffocating with pleasure. She touched him. Touched his sack which nudged her with each stroke and she spread her legs so wide that it seemed she would tear herself open as he continued to plunge into her, as his hands, his lips moved across her body, clawing at her ass, suckling at her nipples.

She stroked his head, clenched her own breasts so hard that pain filled them and then there was no way to endure it, no way to stop the frantic driving of her pelvis against his, to stop the dam from bursting and she came completely undone, gasping with the exertion of fulfillment, falling slack and empty as he finished, nearly lifting her from the earth with the motion of his so-rigid erection, with that untiring wedge which had split her wide, conquered her and now suddenly halted, held poised by its master as it filled her with sweet, fluid satisfaction, with forgetfulness.

If he had mastered her, she had found a way to master him as well, and she clung to him, fulfilled, happy, thrilled with her body's perfect functioning.

His kisses were still sweet and soft. This master of the mysteries held her to him as if she were the dearest thing on earth, and at that moment she was, and at that moment, there was no more satisfied creature on the earth than Julie Shandy.

12.

It was bitter cold in the tunnel. Shelter, chilled all day, exhausted by the efforts of the past week worked feverishly. Julie helped, or tried to, but she was scarcely able to keep her feet.

They may as well have been trapped in an ice cavern. As darkness had fallen outside the cold had penetrated the stone walls of the Shandy mine and now it clutched at them as they worked in darkness, stacking the stones they had gathered higher.

"Shell?"

"Yes." He turned toward her.

"Nothing." A rock clattered onto the pile. "I just wanted to make sure you were still here. This darkness—it's getting to me, I think."

"We'll be out in a little while."

"Yes," Julie answered.

Her voice reflected little confidence. Just then Morgan wasn't too sure himself. They knew there was a way down, but a way up and out was not the same thing. It was like the pit—tumbling in was no problem whatsoever. It was the getting out which was difficult, and it was only the getting out that mattered.

Shelter felt his way to the rockpile and gingerly crept up it, his hands braced against the wall of the shaft.

"Shell!" Julie's voice was nearly panicked.

"I'm just giving it a try. There must be some sort of handhold here."

He eased his way to the top of the pile of rubble and slipped his head and shoulders into the narrow crevice above. His hands searched the smooth stone walls of the shaft, finding nothing to grip.

He looked up, feeling the cold wind in his face. The air was damp and he guessed it was raining above again.

"I think I can make it," Shell said without turning his head.

"You found a way?"

"No, but the shaft is narrow. I should be able to wedge myself in."

"But if you fall . . ."

"We'd be no worse off," Shell said grimly.

He had started to try it, bracing himself with his hands preparing to pull himself up and into the fissure. But Julie called to him.

"Shell. Wait."

"What's the matter?"

"Come down a minute. Please!" Her voice was taut with emotion and he couldn't bring himself to refuse her. With a sigh he slipped back down, finding her in the darkness.

"Hold me, touch me one more time. There—for good luck. Touch me deeply."

He held her for a long moment, feeling the trembling in her shoulders. She was so womanly at times it

152

was difficult to remember just how young she was. He figured he had five minutes to offer her, and he stood there, holding her tightly, his hand warm against her crotch.

"It's time," he said finally. As an afterthought he handed Julie his shirt which was hardly drier than it had been hours ago, but she had nothing.

"All right." She said it quietly. Her hands fell away from his shoulders in the darkness as he turned and returned slowly to the crevice.

It was a tight fit for his shoulders and Shell had much less confidence in this project than he had let Julie see. He slipped his hands up overhead and braced himself and then, shoving off with his feet he was up into the shaft, his legs dangling free.

His shoulders cramped as he felt for fresh purchase and creeping up, waggling his shoulders from side to side he managed only eighteen inches or so. But it was the most important eighteen inches of all.

Now his feet were into the shaft and with his toes digging into the cold stone he was able to shove himself up a foot at a time, his back and palms wedging him into the tight confines.

He could see nothing whatsoever, and the stone rubbed him raw foot and hand, shoulder and hip. If it got much narrower than this, Shell knew he was never going to make it up, knew that he and Julie would spend eternity below, locked in the tomb of stone.

But he didn't allow himself to dwell on that—there was no point in being negative. He simply inched upward, his feet moving up slightly, holding enough to allow him to wriggle his shoulders up another foot.

Suddenly he lost his grip. Rotting stone where he

had planted his feet gave way and he skidded down roughly, tearing the meat from his shoulders and hands.

He heard Julie scream as he skidded to a halt, his eyes stinging with sweat, his chest bathed with perspiration. His hands were raw, but there was no time to stop and lick his wounds. He crept upward again.

Twice more he slipped, once nearly losing it completely, and by then he was high enough so that he knew he would break both legs if he fell to the mine floor.

Each time he somehow continued, feeling dogged determination growing. He was damned if he would let Middlesex get away with this! Kill two young women, take away the mine an old man had worked a lifetime for.

No. Someone would die, but it would be James Middlesex, the criminal and not the innocents.

He hardly thought about his climbing now. It had become mechanical, his body learning what was required of it and doing it.

He simply braced his feet, shoved, locked his shoulders in position, drew his feet up again and shoved. Suddenly his head rapped against something hard enough to set his ears to ringing.

Panting, Shelter swiveled his head, peering up, but he could see nothing. Water trickled down into his eyes to mingle with the hot perspiration which streamed down his throat.

Bracing himself with his right hand he reached up. Planking! That was it—the other entrance. He was an arm's length away from being out, into the free, cold air.

He struck out with the heel of his hand and nothing happened. He struck again, jarring his shoulder. A few drops of muddy earth fell into his face.

It was stuck good. Either nailed down to a rough frame or possibly heaped with soil. It it was the latter Shell had gained nothing by this climb, nothing at all. His heart sunk to the depths, then rose with an angry surge. He was damned if he'd be stopped now! Not if he had to gnaw his way through the planking.

Logic told him that it was better to try knocking an end of the plank free than to bang away at the center of it. Leaning back, his legs drawn up as high as he could lift them, trembling as he trusted his entire weight to them, he lifted both hands and hammered at the end of one of the planks. He thought it moved, but could not be sure.

Stone bit into his back at the wingbones and spine, his legs were cramped, he was drenched with sweat. Mud dripped down continually from above.

Again he struck out and again, with the strength of desperation. From time to time Julie called up to him, her voice seemingly miles distant, but he ignored her—he hadn't the strength to shout back.

Again he struck at the plank with the heel of his hand which was bloody now from his attempts to knock the plank free. He was ready to hang his head, to surrender, to let himself fall, but there was something in the man which had never let him admit defeat, never let him give up and he drove himself, slamming his hand into the plank time and again, smashing bone against wood, hearing a splintering which might well have been his hand and not wood.

He struck out again and his hand went through!

He shook his head and looked up in disbelief. Rain fell into his face. Sweet, cold rain and he felt his heart leap.

He reached up, gripped the splintered end of the plank and tore it free, letting it drop through the crevice, clattering off the stone walls.

The second plank, perhaps weakened by his earlier pounding came free moments later and Shelter gripped the edges of the opening he had battered through the hatch and drew himself up.

His head emerged into the rainy night. Thunder echoed from far away and his head was lashed with rain—nothing could have felt better.

Looking around cautiously he saw that he was in the timber above and to the north of the main entrance to the Shandy mine. He saw no one.

He eased himself up and out, panting hotly as the rain streamed down, as the wind cooled his exertion-heated body.

He rolled to one side of the hatch, lying on the earth, watching the rain fall from the black and stormy skies, watching the big pines sway in the wind. He lay there filling his lungs with the clean air of freedom.

Slowly his body cooled and his breathing slowed. The small sounds which had been reaching his ears for some time through the racket of the storm now took on definition. Julie was shouting.

He rolled over and called down the shaft:

"I'm out. Hold on, I'll find some way of getting you up."

That too was easier said than done and he knew that Julie was going through torment below not knowing when, how, if he would be able to pull her up and out of that pit.

Rising, Shelter searched the woods, finding a long barkless pine branch. It was all of twenty feet long, but that was not long enough. Julie was down twice that distance.

If he could get several of them and tie them together somehow—could she climb that far? There was no way of knowing. But she would have to try it.

He returned to the shaft briefly to call down and re-assure her, then he set out through the rain searching for two more stout, heavy branches.

He returned to the crevice and set about binding them together, end to end, using his jeans which he tore into strips.

It was a hell of a contraption to rely upon, but the canvas of those jeans was heavy, and the pole would be at a slight angle. He could do one thing more to make it easier for Julie and now, squatting in the rain, naked and cold he went about it.

He ripped up the planks and pounded their rusty nails free with a fist sized stone. Then, breaking each plank in half, he nailed them as crosspieces onto the poles. It was time consuming and the finished product wouldn't have done credit to a moronic ape as far as appearance went.

But it had only to function. Once. If she kept a part of her weight against the walls of the crevice she should be able to make it. He tried to call instructions down to her, telling her to brace the end of the pole in the mound of rocks, explaining how she would have to climb, not trusting all of her weight at any time to the jerry-built ladder.

Maybe she understood, maybe she didn't. There was no answer at all from the darkness of the shaft and

157

Shelter could only lower away, hoping against hope that she had heard him, that the contraption would hold her slight weight.

The pole vanished into the shaft with only two feet to spare projecting.

"Julie!" he called, cupping his hands to his mouth as he bent low over the crevice. "Come on up now. Like I told you."

Nothing. There was no reply, no movement of the pole. He had a sudden vision of her just sitting helplessly on the floor of the cave, afraid to try it. In that case he would have to go down after her, although how he would get her up again he had no idea.

"Julie!"

He saw the end of the pole quiver finally. It twitched hesitantly and he could imagine Julie testing her weight, slowly, untrustingly moving up into the crevice, moving inch by inch toward freedom.

Shelter's heart gripped his chest like a fisting hand. If she fell . . . he could only squat against the cold earth, watching the rain roar down across the mountains, watching the pole sway from time to time, mentally trying to lift her, to urge her on, to bring her safely up.

Her hand flashed white against the darkness and Shell's hand shot out, locking around her wrist.

And then she was up and out and they collapsed together against the muddy earth as the cold rain beat down. Julie clung to him, and she started laughing. Laughing long and hard with the joy of being alive.

He held her closely, stroking her hair, and the rain fell.

There was little time for the relief of joy and laughter, however and it struck Shell first. He went rigid and sat up scowling.

"What's the matter?" Julie asked, panting. She held her side which ached from laughing.

"Now what?" Shelter asked soberly. "We're alive, but how long will we last? We've got a dozen armed men below, and we're defenseless."

He looked down at his naked body and suddenly the rain felt colder. "It's got to be done tonight—whatever we can do. Tonight."

"I can't . . ." she objected but Shelter cut her off.

"We've got to get up and move. Try and find your father if possible."

"If my father sees me with you, like this, *he'll* be the one to kill you."

"He's liable to be anyway," Shelter said thoughtfully. "Because like it or not I'm setting D.D. free."

"We'll tell Pa to let her go. Then it will be over, and we can stay together. I'll be wealthy one day, Shell. That's what Pa says."

"Yes." He pet her hair, not mentioning the obvious. She might have been wealthy. That was before James Middlesex came to Massacre. Shelter stood to embrace Julie briefly. He stared off toward Massacre itself, invisible in the darkness and the storm.

Something had to be done and done before first light revealed their presence, or Middlesex could simply cut them down.

"Come on," he said.

"Where to?" Her eyes searched him.

"Down there," he said and Julie too turned to look toward the ghost town.

159

13.

The rain paused sometime after midnight. Shelter couldn't be sure exactly what time it was—the clouds obscured his vision of the stars; but there had been lights in the barbershop the Middlesex gang had appropriated until an hour or so ago. Now the building was dark. A single guard walked the sloppy, water-bright street.

"They're not expecting any more trouble," Shell commented.

"You're not really going down there?" Julie whispered anxiously.

"If there's another way, Julie, I don't know what it is. We've nowhere to run, nowhere to hide. The only chance is to take it to them."

They lay quietly on the slope for long minutes, shivering with the cold. Nothing moved in the town but the lone guard. No lights shone anywhere up the canyon. The Shandy house was dark and still and Shelter wondered if the old man had gotten away.

Or had Middlesex killed him? And what of D.D.?

There were no answers, and it was not the time for

thinking, it was time for acting. Sucking in a deep breath Shell slowly rose to his knees.

Julie watched him, biting her lip but saying nothing.

Time to play Injun, Morgan, he told himself. But he had seen few Indians so ill prepared. He kissed Julie lightly on the lips and then was gone, slipping through the shadows, down the muddy slope, keeping low and to cover, his eyes fixed on the guard who stalked the main street of Massacre.

His town. The idea struck Shell and he smiled in the darkness. Marshal of Massacre. Marshal of an outlaw town, which if cleaned up would belong only to the ghosts again.

The rain had begun once more, drifting down in swirling gusts. The wind was very cold on his back. Lightning struck very far away, paling the northern skies briefly. Distant thunder followed on its heels.

Shell was at the edge of the woods, watching as the guard approached him through the rain. He pulled back behind a wind battered pine, waiting. The guard reached the end of the street and turned his back, starting away from Shell.

He waited until his view of the sentry was cut off by the nearest building, a gray, dilapidated gunsmith's shop. Then Morgan sprinted across the open ground between himself and the building, his bare feet soundless on the sodden earth.

He pressed against the wall of the building in the rain and darkness, wondering—not for the first time these last few days—what kind of madman he was. He had no gun, no knife; but a rock is as good a weapon at close quarters as anything man has ever devised. He searched the ground and found one which nestled nicely in his hand.

Then there was nothing to do but wait. To stand naked in the driving rain, like a man from the stone age. And out there was a nest of saber toothed tigers, up on the ridge his woman.

He heard a sucking sound and another—the sound of a man's boots being pulled from the mud, and he pressed more tightly against the wall of the building, waiting.

Suddenly the man appeared, mechanically plodding, his collar turned up to the weather, hat tugged low.

Shelter moved, the thought uppermost in his mind that this had to be quickly and efficiently done. If the sentry should cry out Shelter was sunk, and with him D.D., Shandy and Julie.

He did not cry out. Shell was on him like a deadly shadow and he brought the rock down sharply on the outlaw's skull, catching him before he could fall. He dragged him behind the building, his eyes flickering up the silent street.

Then, with his heart pounding he lifted the outlaw's gun, yanked off his clothes which fit horribly, and dressed. Rolling the outlaw under the gunshop Shelter stepped into the street himself.

He had done half of what he wanted to do—he had a gun, he had clothing. No matter that the boots floated around on his feet, that the buffalo coat stunk.

Now for the other half—find James Middlesex and take him.

But where? He knew they were using the barbershop as a barracks but he doubted Middlesex, always the aristocrat, would share accommodations with his hired guns.

162

A dark figure suddenly loomed before Shell and he sidestepped hastily, slipping through the open door of the old assayer's office. He was instantly enveloped in cobwebs. They hung everywhere like webbed fog.

He stepped aside, holding the captured pistol near his ear.

"Sam?" the voice outside called. The man grumbled and walked on. He came nearer Shell's position, boots clicking against the ancient boardwalk.

"Sam?"

He didn't cry out again. Shelter slipped out the glassless window of the assayer's office and was behind the man in three quick steps, the muzzle of the Colt coming down on the man's head.

He dragged the outlaw into the assayer's office and moved on, his eyes searching the deserted town through the rain.

He could see the barbershop across the street and beyond it the heap of ashes and blackened timbers of the old saloon.

And then there was another light.

Directly ahead of him a lantern burned low in a small never-painted frame building. Once the general store, Shell recalled from Shandy's town map.

He sidestepped into the alley beside the general store, squatting low, his head constantly moving, aware of the danger all around. He heard a voice and taking a chance he crept nearer to the window which was covered with oil cloth.

Peering in he saw nothing but vague silhouettes. The oilskin was weather tight but for visibility glass had it beat all to hell.

But he could hear well enough, and he recognized

one voice in that back room. He stood near the door in the back alley, listening for a long while, trying to figure out how many men were in that room. Of course there could be a dozen sleeping while two talked, but somehow Shelter didn't think that was the case.

Lightning flashed nearer as the storm moved in with greater intensity from off the dark northern mountains. Water ran in a sheer, silvery fringe from the eaves. Shell put his boot to the latch of the door, kicked out and went in.

He caught the guard by complete surprise and as he lunged for his rifle propped up against the wall, Shelter stepped in, tripped him with a boot and caught him on the jaw with a crushing right hook which put out his lights.

The guard skidded across the plank floor on his chin and stopped against the wall, out cold. Shelter turned quickly to the other man in the room.

"Untie me, marshal," Jack Shandy said.

Shandy was bound hand and foot to an ancient chair. His face was marked up pretty well. An egg sized lump threatened to burst the hide above his eye. His face had been cut, and his mouth showed traces of old blood.

"Where's D.D.?" Shell demanded as he cut the ropes. "Where's Middlesex?"

"Gone. Gone together to Tucson."

"What about. . . ?" Shell demanded angrily.

"Casco's dead. Middlesex killed him, took the girl and tied me up. He had me sign away my claim." Shandy rubbed his sore wrists and then tapped a finger against his battered face. "I didn't give in easy, but what the hell could I do. They said they'd kill Julie."

"He didn't have Julie," Shelter had to tell him and

164

the old man muttered a rare curse.

"Is she all right then?"

"Alive. Cold and tired, but alive." An open trunk in the corner caught Shell's eye. He walked to it, frowning. It was full of woman's clothes.

"D.D.'s stuff. Her husband brought it up here."

Shelter started digging through it and Shandy shouted: "What in hell are you doing? We've got to get out of here!"

"I know a needy girl," Shell said, not turning. He snatched up a calico dress, a pair of high, button shoes, the warmest coat he could find. Rolling them into a bundle he nodded to Shandy.

"Let's pull out, Jack. I've had a belly full of Massacre."

He blew the lamp and they slipped out into the alley. It was still silent. The rain beat down. They walked eastward, into the dark hills, and then made a slow half circle back toward the west where Julie still waited.

Or he hoped she did. He hoped she had done nothing foolish.

Shandy followed Morgan silently, his raspy breathing audible above the sound of the rain. They filtered through the timber, climbing higher. Still Massacre slept. If anyone had noticed the missing guards, no one had come out to check.

They found Julie huddled naked in the cold night and she flew into her father's arms. He held her like a child, murmuring to her and only after a long minute did it seem to dawn on him that she was undressed.

"Morgan!" The old man's voice trembled.

"All in the line of duty, Mayor," Morgan assured

him. He handed Julie the clothing he had brought back. "We'll explain it later. Right now we need to find a place for you to hole up."

"Where are you going?" Julie demanded, pausing, the dress nearly over her hips.

"Tucson, it looks like."

"Why?" Her voice reflected exhaustion and frustration.

Shell explained about D.D. and Middlesex. "He's got your father's half of the mine now. All he needs is for D.D. to go into the recorder's office in Tucson and sign her name. Then he'll have it all. And that'll be the end of the line for D.D."

"I'm going with you," Julie announced, walking towards them.

"No you are not. Definitely not," Shelter said, gripping her shoulders. "Tell her, Shandy."

"No, Julie. Not this time."

"Is there a place you can hole up?" Shell wanted to know.

"The old cabin. The one Ken Short and me threw up back along Beaver Run. None of these yahoos could know about it."

"Good. I've got to get back down there and snatch a horse somehow," Shelter said, looking toward the town. He was wondering just how far he could stretch his luck.

"I know where Casco left his pony," Shandy said. "Take it—it beats trying to slip down into Massacre again."

It did that. Shelter had seen enough of Massacre to last him a lifetime. He looked down upon its gray, jumbled form through the rain once more. It had been deserted, set fire to, torn apart for firewood, dynamited and still with unreasoning tenaciousness the town stood.

Shandy touched his shoulder. "Let's go."

Shell nodded, turned and followed Shandy and Julie through the woods. Shandy knew every rabbit run and rock in those hills, not surprisingly, and it made a difference. They followed a corrugated high ridge where the wind gusted, slapping at them and the rain sliced down like silver sabers.

The horse, Shandy told him, was on the way to the old shack. They came suddenly upon it. In a small thicket a bark and pole shack stood and tethered there was a paint pony.

"Casco's place," Shandy said out loud. He stood looking the place over. "He never would live with us. He was a proud man. He was a Cibecue Indian, Morgan. Stolen from his family by the Apaches when he was just a youngun. They treated him like a dog.

"After that raid the Apache made on Massacre I got into a tussle with an Apache. Luckily I killed him. I say luckily because he was a big, lithe man, almighty strong with wilderness living, and good with a knife." Shandy paused remembering. "We locked together and toppled over. The Indian's head knocked against a rock. It was sheer happenstance, but it killed him. When I got up, shaky and bloody, I seen the kid. A boy not more'n eight, nine. It was Casco, and he'd seen it. He thought I was a great warrior to have killed the evil He-Who-Has-No-Name, the Apache. So I took the boy and raised him. He'd stay with me through the day, but never at night—he was a wild thing, and a good man."

167

The rain had halted. Shandy's eyes met those of Shell, and there were tears standing in them. Or maybe it was Shell's imagination, it could have been the rain.

"The cabin's up over the knoll—you'll never find it, but when you come back . . ." he paused, not saying "if you come back", "we'll be there, and I reckon we'll see you comin', marshal."

"Shell!" Julie fell into his arms and kissed him. "Don't go. She's not worth it, I tell you! Tell him, Pa. Tell him D.D.'s not worth it. Tell him to stay with us."

"I guess the man knows his own mind, Julie. I guess the man knows what he has to do."

Shelter figured he did. He slipped onto the back of the Indian pony, and glancing once at Julie who stood defeated in the rain, at old Jack Shandy whose eyes were still distant, melancholy, he spun the horse around and digging his heels into the paint's ribs, he rode through the deep brush, cresting the high ridge as a broad, deep crimson arrow of dawn pierced the gray clouds to the east.

He sat the pony on top of the ridge for a moment, glanced back once toward Massacre and then rode onto the muddy mountain trail, urging the Indian pony on, toward Tucson where a bloody handed murderer awaited.

14.

The rain settled in again sometime after noon, but Shell no longer needed good tracking weather. He had cut Middlesex's sign early in the morning—they couldn't have had two hour's start on him. Middlesex expected no pursuit. He had left Shelter Morgan buried alive in the Shandy mine and there was no one else.

Their tracks had not been covered in the slightest. They revealed a bold confidence. They were sticking to the Sutler's Flats road, the three of them. Middlesex, D.D. and one gunhand to side James Middlesex. Who he was did not matter. He was simply a man with a gun, a man whose psychology revolved around money, acquiring it and spending it easily, a man who rode with intense loyalty beside the man with the money.

A gap appeared in the clouds overhead and brilliant sunlight streamed through, glittering on the water which ran from every wash, which formed jewels on the grass and on the brush along the trail. The day smelled clean, good. The earth had refreshed itself and marked a new beginning.

Shelter was able to enjoy those thoughts, to remark the beauty of the morning, of the empty land before him without ever forgetting Middlesex, without forgetting that a dying time was coming.

It was his time or Middlesex's time—there could be no other way. True, if he could capture Middlesex, the man could be tried and locked up for many years for his crimes, but Middlesex would never surrender. He would fight, claw and gouge, bite and slash, as would Shelter. As would Shelter Morgan.

The clouds were higher now and Shell could look out onto the desert where already the sands had soaked up the water which had fallen from the skies. The desert seemed implacable, primitive, eternal.

And it was on that desert that Shelter's blood would be spilled. His or Middlesex's. Spilled and soaked up greedily by the white sands, as they had devoured the waters.

It was already growing dark, the skies clearing to reveal brilliant stars, when Shell hit Sutler's Flats. He had hope, but feeble hope that Middlesex might decide to put up for the night in this parasite town.

But Shelter had judged correctly. Middlesex was too hungry for his gold, too impatient to stop here. There was no sign of them anywhere.

But they had changed horses. The hostler at the Arizona Stables remembered. "Sure, Mister Middlesex, his wife and Tex Chambers. Say, Mister," he asked, "what's going on up in them hills? I'm ready to pull out of this hole, but if there's a new gold strike like folks are whisperin', why I reckon I'd stay on for a while."

"I wouldn't listen to folks' gossip," Shell answered. Then he switched the paint for a stubby little roan with a deep chest, one white stocking and a narrow blaze on his nose. "But then again," Shell said as he stepped into leather, "Who knows? I guess there's always a possibility of the town comin' to life again, isn't there? Maybe it'd be a good idea to give it a little time."

He winked at the hostler, shoved his hat down over his eyes and walked the roan out onto the sloppy main street of Sutler's Flats.

He stepped into the saddle and rode past the saloon which was unusually quiet, even for a dying town. The general store which sat on the corner of the main street and an apparently seldom used trail leading off into the southern hills was still lighted.

Shell swung down, walked across the muddy plankwalk and went in. It took a few minutes dickering but he managed to trade one of the handguns he was carrying for a sack of sugar, coffee, bacon and ammunition.

"Nobody's got hard cash," the elderly clerk sighed as he tucked the Colt away. Five dollars was the most he could give, but it was enough for what Shelter needed.

"By the way, seen that James Middlesex?" Shell asked as he was almost to the door.

"Him. . . !" Disgust curled the clerk's lips. He removed the expression immediately, glancing with trepidation at the tall, broad shouldered man before him.

"I feel that way too," Shelter told the man. "I'm looking for him, but I'm not one of his men." The clerk hesitated. "I'm the marshal from up in Massacre," Shell said.

"Massacre?" the clerk looked at him as if he were mad.

"I know," Shell said. "It's not much of a town, but Jack Shandy figured we needed us a lawman suddenly.

I was appointed."

"Took the southern route not more'n two, three hours ago." The clerk spoke rapidly, softly as if afraid of being overheard.

"His wife with him?" Shell asked. The clerk nodded.

Shell went out into the cold night and as he was tying the sack to his saddle he glanced up to see the clerk, his apron fluttering in the wind.

"Something else?" Shelter asked.

"No . . . I just wanted to say this: You ever get Massacre cleaned up and you're still looking for that kind of work, why we've got plenty that needs to be done right here in Sutler's Flats."

Then he turned and went in, closing the door behind him. Shell nodded thoughtfully, smiled and stepped up, settling into the saddle of the roan.

"Let's hit that trail, pony," he said to the horse, "we've got a ride ahead of us."

For a few minutes, leaving town, with the lights of Sutler's Flats on the trail, he could see the deeply imprinted tracks of the three horses ahead of him, and then the darkness swallowed up the trail. The sky was roofed over with clouds once more, although a small pocket of stars appeared intermittently off to the south.

He felt fine, he decided. The exhilaration of the chase was in him. It was a cool night and he had a good horse beneath him and a gun at his belt.

Not that he didn't have his share of physical aches. If he dwelled on them it was positively unnerving. His head, after all these days, still ached. He had a badly bruised and lacerated hand, contusions on his back, a twisted ankle.

None of that mattered much right now. The land was

slowly flattening. The gorge he rode through opened onto the dead sea of the wide desert. The roan moved fluidly beneath him, and somewhere, perhaps on this very night, he would face down the murderer.

He thought with a twinge of guilt and apprehension of D.D., but he knew that Middlesex would not kill her now until she had signed away her birthright in Tucson.

And by Tucson it would all be over—one way or the other. He worried about her in another way. Say Middlesex used her as a shield, what then? If it came to D.D.'s safety or capturing Middlesex. It would have to be the girl he thought of first, of course, and only that lingered to nag Shelter as the horse loped out onto the desert flats, and Shell saw the trio of tracks ahead of him stretched out in a straight line toward the southwest, toward Tucson.

He rode on through the night, past the silent sentinels of saguaro cactus, their arms thrust up toward the dark skies as if in a gesture of surprise.

As the hours passed the burst of exhilaration he had felt began to wane and he rode somberly, struggling with weariness. He must be alert when he met Middlesex and his gunhand, Tex Chambers. His life and D.D.'s would depend on it.

Initially he had imagined Middlesex would hole up in Sutler's Flats for the night, then later he had decided the man would camp somewhere after leaving town. He had done neither.

The man was riding almost as if he knew someone was pursuing him, and yet he couldn't. Gold spurred Middlesex on, gold had driven him to murder, gold dominated his thoughts, and it seemed it was his life.

What had he done in between the night of the

slaughter, that night along the bloody Conasauga River in Georgia and the day he had decided to steal the Shandy mine? There was no telling, of course, but Shelter imagined he had fervently pursued his personal salvation, a salvation which could only be purchased with gold.

How many others had he tormented and killed in his mad pursuit? How many would he kill if he escaped this time or proved to be better, or luckier, with a gun than Morgan.

Shelter rode on, slowing the roan to a walk to conserve its energy. After midnight they crossed a wash where water, racing white, ran off the distant mountains, and Shelter paused to let the horse drink its fill.

Hours more passed and his head jerked up. He realized that he had fallen asleep in the saddle and knew it was no good to continue like this. He didn't want to meet Middlesex with frayed nerves, heavy eyelids, weary muscles.

He ground tethered the horse, using a heavy flat rock to hold the reins and curled up in a blanket to sleep. Only for an hour he told himself, only an hour as the cold night passed.

He couldn't know that over the next dune, less than a quarter of a mile away, James Middlesex had made his own camp.

Shell was up with the sunrise; the air was crisp, utterly still and clear beneath a mantle of high, scudding clouds.

Not fifteen minutes later he found the abandoned camp and he slowly, methodically cursed himself. The roan twitched its ears and rolled shocked eyes toward this new rider.

"Almost," Shell grumbled to the horse. "I could have had him. Another half an hour last night and I would have had the bastard."

He got down and examined the tracks briefly. Three people. Two men and a woman. He could see where their bedrolls had been spread in the soft sand; touching their burned out fire he could still feel warmth. They were less than an hour ahead now. Less than an hour—he looked across the desert which was oddly blue beneath the clouds and toward the barren, rocky hills which were beginning to shoulder up to the west.

Then, swinging into leather, his face grim, he kneed the horse into a canter, swinging toward the hills to parallel himself with their trail.

It was better to come up on them from an unexpected angle. A man arriving from behind would be studied with the closest scrutiny, one from the opposite direction would be assumed to be a passerby until he proved otherwise—and Shell decidedly meant to prove otherwise.

The day grew warm, muggy as he rode closer to the mountains. A breeze had arisen and it whipped sand before it, depositing it on the chocolate flanks of the mountains.

He looked to their heights, seeing no sign of timber or grass. Water still rushed off the mountains, but it raged down the gulleys without settling or soaking in. It had the effect of washing away anything that grew rather than nourishing it.

He drifted the roan toward higher ground now, passing through a stand of nopal cactus which covered several acres. The horse picked its way through and climbed higher.

Shelter held the roan up after he had gained some elevation and, squinting out onto the desert he searched for the three riders.

Nothing.

They were nowhere to be seen and Shelter, frowning deeply, moved the horse ahead a way, following a natural trail along the contours of the low mountains.

He made a bend, dipped down into a ravine where a foot of water raced past, climbed again and once more halted the roan and again searched the desert basin, this time more carefully, with infinite patience, his eyes working in a fixed pattern.

Nothing.

Had they turned away then, ridden east or south across the vast desert? For what purpose. Middlesex wanted only to reach Tucson. Nothing else mattered.

The only alternative answer was that they had ridden into the mountains themselves, reaching the hills before Shelter himself had.

That bothered him. Why go into the mountains? True it was a little shorter route, but no quicker. Could they have seen Shelter and decided to take to the mountains for safety? Unlikely, but possible. More possible and chilling was the knowledge that Middlesex was now above him, and from there he could definitely have seen Shell.

He rode on slowly, making the assumption that he had been spotted. Middlesex knew he was coming now and it was suddenly a different game.

Half a mile on he found the trail. Three horses had ridden up from the flats, the same three horses. Following them a way, his eyes going warily to the higher slopes, Shelter found a spot where the horses had milled and halted. A man had gotten down.

Oh, they knew all right. They knew now.

Middlesex was definitely no fool. His idea in going into the mountains was exactly this—to be able to look out for mile upon mile across the desert and study the land for any sign of pursuit.

Shelter breathed a slow curse. What was there to do but follow them into those hills? To circle the mountains would take an extra day, a day in which Middlesex could reach Tucson, take care of business at the recorder's office and hire as many thugs as it took to take care of Shelter Morgan.

He patted the roan's neck and turned it upslope, his eyes on the trail ahead of him, a trail where death awaited.

He was wary, but not expecting trouble just yet. There was no decent cover anywhere on these slopes. The three horses he was following plodded on at an even pace, their tracks easy to read. If only he could read the thoughts of this killer that easily.

By late afternoon the trail had steepened. The canyons grew convoluted and the trail blind as it wove its way upward. Shell didn't like the set-up at all now. He had to get off this trail.

He swung the roan up a rock strewn canyon, the horse laboring as Shell urged it upward. Finally they halted, horse and rider bathed in sweat, the cold sundown wind whipping over them, shrieking up the canyons.

And now what? He could see nothing but the broad sweep of the desert, the jumble of mountains stretching out to the north and south.

He was above them, or thought he was. But how fast could he travel off the trail? It had turned into a guessing game, and the stakes were life or death.

15.

Dusk settled slowly. The tall, lean man in the over-sized clothing sat hunched on the tiny ledge on the slope of the stark and barren mountain, watching darkness shade the deep canyons.

He was motionless, arms around his shoulders, the right hand holding the reins to the roan horse which stood beside him, nuzzling him impatiently from time to time. He was motionless except for those icy blue eyes which moved constantly, searching the land which fell away beneath him.

When it was nearly dark he rose and stepped into the saddle of the roan, riding it slowly and silently across the face of the wind-scoured mountain.

He was there, somewhere below—Major James Middlesex, scoundrel, thief, killer. And his time had come.

Sundown had briefly purpled the mountain slopes, had colored the cloudy skies and then the wind had washed away all of the color, the land had faded to a uniform gray, only the tips of the high peaks shining with a dull, metallic red.

He rode downward, slanting toward the west, the

clicking sounds of the roan's hoofs over stone muffled by the roar of the wind.

Shelter stopped abruptly. He saw it distinctly—the red beacon of a small fire, and he smiled.

Middlesex, he knew, had seen him. Then why start a campfire? It could only have the purpose of luring him down.

He ignored the fire. He was within a quarter of a mile of it, riding across a narrow, wooded bench. The cedar smell was rich in the darkness. The trunks of the trees were still damp with the rain.

He paused, on the lip of a ledge and looked out over the entire world. Night shadowed mountains, empty, starlit desert. The fire glowed, summoning him.

The fire meant only one thing to Morgan—they were nearby. Hiding behind rocks, pressed flat against the earth, rifles cool in their perspiration-slick hands.

They were waiting for him. Shell sat the roan a long minute, feeling the cool rush of the wind in his face.

They were waiting.

There was no point in keeping them waiting. He unsaddled the roan and slipped the bit from its mouth. "Go on," he hissed, slapping it on its flank.

They were expecting a man on horseback. The horse's hoofs were audible for long distances. The roan, so necessary hours ago had become a liability.

He watched the horse trot uncertainly away and begin to graze, tugging at the poor cheat grass beneath the cedars, then, shedding his boots, he began to work his way down the slopes.

The clouds, obligingly, were creeping in once more and the mountains were completely dark. Shelter, however, had the beacon of the campfire to draw him down.

179

They were there, somewhere in ambush. It was a challenge and he had accepted it. If their skills were better than his, it would be his bones which were left to bleach on these lonesome desert mountain slopes.

He was gambling that they were not.

He had wriggled up a hillrise slowly, his muscles taut and now he could overlook the campsite. There were three beds made up and what seemed to be human forms inside them. Away from the fire stood two horses.

Where was the third? Shell remained where he was, and with infinite patience he studied the dark hills surrounding the camp. Still he saw nothing to give Middlesex away. There was no glint of starlight on metal, no shifting shadow, and he heard no sharp exhalation of impatient breath.

He rolled away from the rim of the hillrise, letting an hour pass. Let the night lull them, let the cold chill their muscles, let them become impatient or incautious. It was not the time to gamble.

He lay back, heart pounding with adrenalin, trying to quiet himself by breathing slowly, trying to think and move like an Indian.

The dark shadow loomed up suddenly, cutting a stark silhouette against the night sky. A gun blazed away, stabbing crimson daggers at Morgan. He rolled, firing back once, feeling the sudden, fiery pain in his chest.

Tagged! Out-Injuned and outshot. Shell dove headfirst down the rocky slope, tearing his flesh on cactus and stone, rolling away from the deadly guns.

Suddenly it was still. As abruptly as it had begun it was ended. He lay in the cover of tangled manzanita and sage brush, his pulse pounding furiously, his body leaking blood.

How badly was he hit? He didn't even dare move to check that. He only knew it felt as if a mule had kicked him in the chest, knew that quantities of blood were trickling from a wound high in the chest.

He froze, every muscle tense. A slight sound, the whisper of brush against jeans had reached his ears. He knew the man hunting him was cautious. And quite good.

It had to be this Tex Chambers. Shell had seen briefly his lanky silhouette, seen the curl of his hat. It was not Middlesex, but then he wouldn't have expected Middlesex to fight as long as there was someone left to fight, to bleed, to die for him.

He heard another tiny, hesitant sound and he still did not move. He knew what thoughts were going through the hunter's mind now—was Morgan dead, playing possum? He didn't want Shell to slip away in the darkness, nor did he want to pursue too quickly.

Shell closed his eyes tightly for a moment, fighting off the pain which surged through his body, and when he opened them the hunter was there.

He could see nothing of him but a boot, the leather of it gleaming dully in the meager starlight. Shell lay motionlessly, watching, waiting.

In the brush where he lay he knew he must be invisible, but the gunman was liable to drill a couple of shots into the thicket just to be sure.

He saw the man turn, saw his boot toes pointed directly at him and less than ten feet away. Shell slowly brought his Colt around, moving it inch by inch until its muzzle was trained on the man's legs.

The hammer was already back, he had only to elevate the gun barrel and squeeze.

181

As he did the thunder of his .44 split the night. Flame splashed from the muzzle, momentarily blinding Shell with its light. He fired, heard the outlaw scream and he lunged from the brush, a savage thing in the night.

Hair hung in his eyes, blood streamed from his chest and rage burned in his heart. He fired again from three feet away, and without waiting to see where the bullet hit, he slammed a shoulder into the outlaw's chest, wanting to take him down, to prevent a desperate shot from tearing into his own body.

Shell hit him and they toppled over. They slid together down a flat, sloping stone the size of a table and together, locked in fierce mortal combat, they fell over the rim of the outcropping toward the floor of the gulley thirty feet below.

They slammed to the earth, Shell feeling with anger and frustration, his Colt being jarred free of his grip.

Chambers, whatever else the outlaw might have been, was no coward. And he could fight. That fall from the cliff should have taken the fight out of him, but it seemed only to infuriate him.

He was at Shell with fists and boots, trying to throw him off. Shell took a sharp right hand to the temple and countered. He smashed his forearm against Chambers' nose, and blood flecked both of them. Chambers fought back, bringing a knee up hard against Shell's groin and Shell, curling up with pain, felt himself rolled aside.

As they stood he could see that Chambers too had lost his weapon in the fall. The outlaw stood facing Shell, hands dangling, chest rising and falling with exertion. Shell was doubled up still, feeling the nausea boil in his abdomen.

Still he was quick enough to move aside as Tex Chambers kicked out viciously. His boot grazed Shell's hip as he turned away, then spinning back, Shell threw himself at Chambers, swinging a wild right.

Chambers took it on the chin, and backed away. But he fought on.

Chambers tried again to land a kick on Shell's kneecap, just missing as Shell pulled away. Morgan, still in agony from the knee to the groin, nevertheless moved in. He wasn't going to win backing away, and to lose was to forfeit his life.

He reached out suddenly and grabbed Chambers by the front of his shirt, yanking him off balance and into a left hook which shook the outlaw to his toes.

Chambers clawed at Shell's eyes, trying to gouge them out of his skull, but Shell, wagging his head from side to side evaded the digging fingers although Chambers' nails raked his cheek, drawing blood.

Chambers had his chin up and Shell struck out viciously, his fist slamming into the outlaw's throat. Shell felt cartilage give, saw Chambers clutch at his own throat as he gasped for breath. Strangling, the wide-eyed gunhand dove at Shell, trying to butt him with his skull. Shelter sidestepped and tripped the man, and it was only as Chambers hit the ground that Shell's eyes caught the dull gleam of the pistol which lay not ten inches from Chambers' hand.

The outlaw had seen it too and as Shell moved in Chambers spun and from his back he fired. The bullet went up Shell's pantleg and out the fabric at the knee, hitting nothing as Shell's foot slammed into Chambers' hand, knocking the pistol free once more.

Shell kicked out again, his bare heel catching the

outlaw above the eye. Then again he kicked him, this time full in the face. Blood spurted from Chambers' mouth and his head snapped back against the earth.

He lay there choking on his own blood, his windpipe strangled off and Shell stood over him, hands limp, shirt torn, heart hammering until with a terrible gurgling sound Chambers ceased to move, ceased to breathe. He lay silently against the cold earth, dead.

Shell moved immediately, knowing the shots might bring Middlesex. He searched frantically for the pistol but could not find it. It had been flung into the brush and was lost. Moving back toward the spot where they had fallen, holding his chest which was torn and bleeding, flooded with pain, he searched the ground for the other pistol. He had the same luck—it too was gone.

Numbly he got down on the ground and searched with his hands. Desperately he groped for it, wasting precious moments. Yet without the pistol he was lost, and he knew it. He was badly wounded and doubted he had the strength to go through another battle of any sort, yet with a Colt in his hand there was always a chance.

A Colt .44 pistol—it became a relic of faith in his mind just then. Salvation, bright promise, hope, life itself all wrapped up in Colonel Colt's assemblage of blue steel and springs, walnut grips and brass screws. It was a savage religion, but one which Shelter had adhered to throughout his life, a religion which never seemed more compelling than it did now.

He saw something—his heart leaped. Perhaps it was only a water bright stone. He started toward it, hoping, but the hope was broken off.

A gun belched fire from the ridge, spattering Shelter with earth, and he turned and crashed into the brush,

184

his hands empty, his search futile.

It was a carbine which sought him, seven rapid shots penetrated the brush, searching left then right, each deadly missile slicing through the brush, tearing up earth and stone within feet of where Shelter lay pressed to the earth, daring not to move.

"You should have stayed in Tennessee, Captain Morgan!" a taunting voice called from somewhere above Shell. He heard the cool, metallic sounds of a rifle being reloaded. "You're going to die tonight, Morgan! Can you hear me?" The voice rose to a shriek, it quivered with anger and mad frustration. "Can you hear me!" And then the firing began again, sightless bullets searching the darkness.

They pinged into the brush, whined off the stone around Shell's head.

"I can sit here all night, Morgan! Doesn't bother me a bit. I've got a box of a hundred rounds here. Do you understand? I'm going to kill you, you're going to die." Three more rounds were spotted into the brush and Shelter knew Middlesex was right. If he stayed where he was he was going to do exactly that—die. Sooner or later one of those rounds, flying blindly through the night would find him, would sever an artery, smash flesh and bone, and Shelter Morgan would live no more.

It was true and it maddened Shell. The bastard would live on, spending his gold, drinking brandy, smoking a cigar as he watched sundown across the skies from the porch of the Short mansion. While Shelter Morgan lay dead, unburied on this godforsaken mountain.

"Morgan!"

Shell did not move. It was still dark, and while it stayed dark he had a chance. But there was a late rising moon and by its thin light Shell, even in the deep brush where he now lay, would be exposed.

A single shot was fired from the ridge and it struck with sudden ferocity. It was no more than three inches from the fingers of his right hand and that hand curled into a fist reflexively as the blood thundered through Shell's brain.

There was a number of small rocks near at hand and taking a chance that his movement might be seen, he winged one far to the left and then another. A third he tossed to his right. None drew a shot, but he now wriggled forward cautiously, hoping that any sound he made might also be disregarded. He had dragged himself all of ten feet when a shot near enough to part his hair smashed into the brush.

He lay there furious with himself, with Middlesex, angry with the night, with the mountains and all of life. It was through that anger that slow determination began to creep.

He might die, be blown to chunks of bloody meat, but he would not simply lie there like a dog awaiting the bullet with eyes, the one which would not miss. The moon would be rising soon, and later the sun. To lie still was to die, to move to die—but in movement there was a chance.

His heart pounding, he bunched his muscles, toes curling up and digging in, ready to shove off. When. . . ? when, it could make all the difference. After he had been silent for a long while, after he had fired a volley . . . when?

There was no good choice. He only knew he had to

move, to run. He tried to recall what the terrain ahead of him looked like and could not.

Now a slow coldness crept through Shell. It came with the determination that he would not remain where he was. It was a strange coolness which calmed his heart, seemed to make his vision grow more acute. The pain in his chest seemed to subside.

He had experienced something like this before, in battle. The soldier's salvation it was called. A knowledge of the imminence of death which seemed somehow to shut out the fear of death.

Shell closed his eyes, briefly resting his forehead against the earth. And then he was up, sprinting wildly through the brush, moving in a weaving crouch, his bare feet tearing themselves against unseen stones and roots, the brambles ripping at his flesh as the bullets flew around him, the rifle on the hillrise barking time and time again.

He was to it suddenly. The wash yawned before him and Shelter hurled himself toward it, heedless of his body.

He crashed through a stand of heavy brush and came up short against a boulder which lay hidden there. The lights went on in Shell's skull, silver and black pinwheels spinning behind his eyes as he slammed into the hidden rock.

He was only half himself, but that half which was alert screamed out with silent urging: Get the hell out of here! He's back there and he's got a gun!

Shell grappled with the brush and got to his feet. Staggering from the brush he found the bottom of the wash, his head swiveling back toward the rim of the gulley. Still no pursuit.

Upslope or down? He chose down just because upslope was a more logical tactic. He crept down it through the deep shadows of the silent night. He had gone three hundred yards when he decided to come back up out of the wash, breaking a trail through the sumac.

Then he was onto open ground and could move more swiftly, more silently, but he could also be seen much more easily. He halted, squatting down to look back along his trail and back up the canyon to where he had last seen Middlesex. Looking he saw nothing; listening he heard nothing.

Weaponless, he was a sitting duck. He had a thought, one which could either end it quickly or save his hide. The camp.

Tex Chambers had carried no rifle, yet he must have had one—was there a man west of the Mississippi who didn't carry one on the plains? No, he must have had one, and logically it would be in the camp, in the scabbard of his saddle.

Of course he could be wrong, maybe Chambers was an odd man, maybe he had been carrying a rifle and had lost it, but to Shell just then, desperate as it was, it seemed his only chance and, having caught his breath, he moved out at a crouch, creeping up the hillside before him, the faint glow of the campfire coloring the sky above the rise.

He threw caution to the winds—none of this was going to help him if Middlesex returned to the camp ahead of him. He broke over the rise and then stopped suddenly.

D.D.—she sat beside the fire, her knees drawn up, arms looped around them, head down. He could not tell if she was tied or not. Probably not; where could she run after all?

He slipped and skidded down the steep incline, and in another minute he was into the camp. He rushed on silent, bare feet across the clearing and D.D.'s face came up with a start.

Her mouth opened soundlessly and then closed again. Her face was utterly pallid, her eyes empty, her mouth dragged down at the corners.

"Shelter!" she finally said in a breathless voice.

"Sh! Get up," he panted. "We're getting the hell out of here."

Already he had spotted it—a Winchester rifle leaning against a well worn saddle twenty feet from where D.D. sat and he strode toward it as D.D. stood limply, her arms dangling.

He was reaching for the rifle when he heard her scream, heard her voice rise to a shrill cry: "Kill him! Oh, God, Kill him!"

Shelter spun, grabbing for the rifle, but it was too late. James Middlesex stood there already, his eyes cold and vicious, a big blue Colt revolver in his hand.

16.

Shelter froze. Maybe he should have kept moving but it seemed useless. He had to reach the rifle, draw it from the scabbard, lever in a cartridge, turn and fire. All James Middlesex had to do was squeeze that curved blue trigger.

They had always said it would happen: "You'll hunt them until one of them kills you, Shelter." How many times had he heard that? He wouldn't be hearing it again.

"Kill him!" D.D. cried again. But she wasn't looking at Shelter, she was looking at her husband. "Kill him, James. Kill the meddling bastard!"

Middlesex was smiling, but it wasn't a nice expression. The skin was drawn taut over his cheekbones, his mouth was frozen, masklike, his eyes glittered in the dull firelight.

"Look at him," Middlesex said. He was savoring it now, feasting on it. "Look at the hero, D.D. Thought you were saving the maiden, did you, Captain?"

Shell was expressionless. He measured the distance

from his hand to the rifle. Too far. Just too damned far.

"Poor little D.D." Middlesex took a step nearer. "Mister Morgan was supposed to stay at the house until we could take care of him. But Morgan wanted to protect little D.D. and he made her go up into the hills. Then that damned Indian snatched her. D.D. wants to be home, sipping brandy, getting rich, don't you D.D.?"

"Why are you talking? Kill him," she said.

"Mister Morgan is wondering how I stumbled on this, aren't you, Mister Morgan?" Middlesex's voice was triumphant. He was enjoying this almost as much as he would enjoy driving that .44 bullet into Shell's heart.

"It was all D.D.'s plan. She found me and said she wanted a man to kill her father—what do you think of that, Mister Morgan? What do you think of our sweet young D.D. now?"

"Are you going to do it or do I have to?" she shrieked.

"Oh, I'm going to do it, dear D.D.," Middlesex answered. "I have to, don't I? If I don't Mister Morgan won't quit until he sees me dead. And I'm just afraid, D.D., that the same can be said for you."

"What?" She turned, eyes angry and wide, but her lips were trembling. "I don't get it."

"Sure you do," Middlesex said. "You hired me to kill your father. What's to stop you from hiring someone else to kill me?"

"Don't be mad," she said, and she tried to laugh, but couldn't manage it. She stepped toward him, arms stretched out. "Darling . . ."

Middlesex's pistol muzzle blossomed into flame. The gun bucked in his hand, snapping his arm up. D.D. simply gurgled and it was not until she turned, falling, that Shelter could see the gaping wound in her chest, the quick spread of crimson across her blouse.

Middlesex, the bastard, was grinning. He turned the pistol on Shell and then simply toppled forward on his face. He lay there, sprawled against the earth, the firelight dancing in his open eyes.

How? Shell hesitated then stepped toward him, kicking the pistol away from Middlesex's hand. He turned him over with his foot and saw the terrible wound from the other gun, the one which had been fired simultaneously with Middlesex's shot.

He was stone dead, his spine crushed by a bullet from a big-bored buffalo gun. Shelter let Middlesex flop back against the ground, and then, stepping around the dead body of D.D. Short, he went to the fire where he sat to wait for Julie to come down off the mountain.